The Book** Prize Winner

Jonathan King

BLAKE

Published by Blake Publishing Ltd,
3 Bramber Court, 2 Bramber Road, London W14 9PB, England

First published in Great Britain 1997

ISBN 1 85782 192 0

British Library Cataloguing-in-Publication Data:
A catalogue record for this book is available
from the British Library.

Typeset by BCP

Printed in Wales by Creative Print and Design (Wales),
Ebbw Vale, Gwent

1 3 5 7 9 10 8 6 4 2

For Ailsa King, 1997

Prologue

The bread and butter pudding was delicious in Harvey Nicks but he wasn't having any of it. He sipped his tepid tea. He prided himself on his powers of observation.

She was clearly a widow. Not divorced. No element of self-assurance. Fattish. Rounded. Elegant in a tasteless kind of way. That suit could have been made out of curtain material. The handbag was leather but probably Harrods. The shoes were polished but last year's model.

Talked a lot. Probably chattered her husband to death. One child. A boy — certainly gay. The way she gestured and dominated the room, she'd clearly mothered the poor lad to the point of sexual suffocation.

He was quite wrong, actually. Not only had she never been married — she'd never been kissed. Even at Roedean, whilst being quite accepted amongst the other girls, she had hardly been popular. Plain but pleasant; quite bright; strolled a lot along the bleak coast, gazing out at the grey, gloomy, turbulent sea, thinking about those romantic stories. Atop the tall white cliffs, as the seagulls wheeled and squealed, dreaming dreams about other characters, other lives, other loves. At dances, nobody had wanted to escort her on to the floor. She'd had friends but no passionate embraces.

As for the man, he was an actor. Wide gestures; loud laughter; dyed hair; tiny hands, little pink things with polished nails and delicate fingers. A thespian. Or perhaps a dancer.

Wrong again. He was a critic, acerbic with pen and acid in review. Playrights had withered beneath his scorn. Yet he was much loved by those he destroyed, possibly because he was often accurate and never malicious. His comments were born from a love of the arts and for that reason he was much forgiven.

An illicit affair, he decided. Possibly both married or re-married. They could only meet here at Harvey Nicks, lunching on the salmon fishcakes in a cream and mushroom sauce, sipping the recommended Vernaccia, Terruzi & Puthud '95 at £4.50 a glass, concluding with the bread and butter pudding with apricot compôte and Jersey cream or a slice of cherry cheesecake and cups of espresso black and then discreetly popping back to his rooms in the Hyde Park

Hotel round the corner for a spot of slap and tickle.

'Why did people like that bother?' he wondered to himself. Clearly well into middle-age, the lusts must have receded years ago. What did he see in her podgy face, the double chins, the wobbly jowls? And why was she so enamoured with his wrinkled skin, bristly jaw and dry lips? Receding white hair uncombed and sticking up in unruly tufts.

And yet there was a charm to it all. *Brief Encounter*. Trevor and Celia. The train station buffet. Black-and-white, with Rachmaninoff in the background, that glorious theme.

As he watched, they smiled and shook their heads.

Clearly they adored each other.

In reality, they were good friends but no more, and their relationship was spiky and jovially antagonistic.

He came here every day just to watch. Take in the individuals, assess the crowd, invent lives for them and then return to his small bed-sitting-room to scribble his unpublished inspirations. One day they would be considered great works.

The waitress filled his teapot with fresh hot water. Of all the customers, he was the meanest. Nobody else could stretch out a smaller order for longer. And always on her station. No tip. He insisted on deducting the cheekily described discretionary service charge of 12.5% that 'will be added to your bill' here on the Fifth Floor. No smile. Sad creature. Pathetic and lonely. And worse than that. Smelly.

She was working-class, he decided. Studied her way through state school, got a job as a secretary, very good at it, married the boss, retired into suburban society, wife and mother, probably in Sutton or Cheam ...

Not so. Born into an reasonably upper-class family, her father had been a successful surgeon after going to public school and Oxford. Her mother was the daughter of a bank manager who rode horses rather well. Their only child, she had been properly raised and educated but neither had ever expressed much interest in her or affection for each other. They politely conformed to life in rural post-War England, after having served respectably in the clerical branches of the services during the conflict, sent her to school, financed her University courses, fed her, clothed her, allowed her to take nominal jobs at the *Guardian* newspaper and then thoughtfully passed away in a motor vehicle accident, leaving her a home, suitable funds and nothing to do.

At that moment, the couple rocked with hysterical glee and he looked away in embarrassment. There were times when he felt ashamed, as though he was prying, snooping, eavesdropping. He poured himself another cup of tea, so weak it looked like yellow water. A drop of milk, unwrapped two lumps of sugar, plopped them into his cup, fumbled for the spoon, examined the crest on the silver handle, stirred well ... and when he looked up again, they had gone.

Now that table over there ... father, mother, son, girlfriend — all just in from India, tourists from Delhi visiting the West End. He wasn't close enough to hear them speaking in Arabic.

He prided himself on his powers of observation.

Part 1

One

$\mathcal{F}$rom tiny acorns, vast tenements can grow.

The statue of David was carved from a solid chunk of marble. Other pieces from the larger rock adorn bathrooms in San Basilio, a suburb of Rome on Via Tiburtina, on the way to the Tivoli Gardens.

Michelangelo had no hand in the creation of those toilet bowls, but the marble started life at the same time, in the same quarry.

These were some of the thoughts engaging Elizabeth Regina as she sat aboard the GB Air jet from Heathrow to Tangier. A portly woman of uncertain age, her iron-grey hair sat smartly on her head above a face of regal appearance, mouth tinted pinkly, eyebrows exquisitely plucked and arched, nose tilted neat and perky, eyes missing not a trick of her fellow passengers' idiosyncratic twitches and gestures.

She'd been asked for her autograph several times. Very polite requests, impeccably delivered as befitted a writer of her status.

Her novels sold in their millions. Around the globe, translated into thousands of foreign languages. Works to tug the ladies' hearts. Stories of noble love and frustration, devoted worship and unfair punishment. Unrequited unselfishness and unrewarded admiration except at the end, when it inevitably all came right.

This was an unusual holiday for Elizabeth Regina. Her planned sojourn in The Canaries with Isobella had been cancelled at the last minute due to unforeseen influenza on her companion's part. Sneezing ruefully down the phone, days of bed insisted upon by the doctor, double-package indemnity insurance called into action and the only option, other than remaining at Willings with the spaniels already booked for the kennels, was one return ticket to Morocco, two weeks of sunshine, full board in a luxury suite at the El Minzah Hotel, where she was assured that the food was edible and the water practically pure.

Elizabeth didn't know much about Morocco. It was Arabic, a monarchy, home to several respected writers, and hot. She regarded the whole thing as a bit of an adventure. On her own — a first. A new land, fresh culture, different sights. She was determined to enjoy herself. And write not a word. The daily grind of rise, shine and churn out 2,000 words could be left behind in Surrey for a fortnight.

The plane shuddered to the ground. Dry, scabby, dusty runway; new but simple bungalow of a terminal, all polished linoleum floors and plastic desks. Interminable queues lined up in front of beaming, child-like immigration officials. Dusky faces, white teeth, hairy hands, sparkling eyes.

There was a lot of noise on the other side of Customs. A teeming mass of Moroccan men, shouting and grabbing and grinning and gesticulating. A sign with the El Minzah logo; a taxi drive through narrow roads at much greater speed than was sensible, past, and occasionally over, wandering sheep.

The hotel was delightful. A Moorish palace with a courtyard, excellent restaurant and good service. She liked the natives. Rowdy and exuberant but well intentioned. The children begging with smiles and cheek. The smell of spices. Everywhere you looked, jellabas and sandals. Foreign but exotic, and the hotel suite was air-conditioned and comfortable with white linen, wooden floors and a subtle smell of pine. 'This will do nicely,' thought Elizabeth Regina, as she dozed off into the Land of Nod.

Breakfast was served by a schoolgirl maid who simpered a lot and appeared to have only a smattering of French. Since Elizabeth was not conversant with a single word of Arabic, the communication was limited to beams and gestures. The eggs were perfectly boiled, four-and-a-half minutes, firm white and runny yolk, in delicious little blue-and-white china cups. The coffee smelled and tasted fresh. The bread rolls were crisp and hot; the butter creamy and salty.

By the time, Elizabeth emerged into the lobby, scrubbed pink and flushed from the bath, she was feeling very positive about Tangier. Strolling up the narrow lane to the big square, she sat at a table outside the huge Café de Paris dominating the thoroughfare, and watched Africa pass by.

All the men flirted with her as they strolled. Twinkling, wicked eyes and dimples all over their faces. The women hurried past, either veiled or demure, except for the Westernised girls, flaunting their jeans and T-shirts in bold defiance. The children asked for coins and chattered and scampered like urchins.

A mustachioed Moroccan in his 20s politely asked if he could sit at her table, spoke in French, Arabic and, mainly, American English, enquired with soft, brown, lash-fringed intensity what she did, how many family members she had, how long she intended to stay and, slipping from phrase to phrase with all the ease of a snake, suggested showing her his cousin's shop in the casbah. Elizabeth, who could be as firm and determined as any English lady, declined in a way which convinced him to give up his task with a chuckle and a shrug.

She walked alone down the hill to the beach-front and strolled along, looking at the bathing tourists and frolicking locals. Lithe brown bodies spun amongst fat pink whales like minnows flirting with sharks. The air smelt of coconut lotion and spices, broiling meat and pungent rubbish. The sand looked white and clean. The individual beach areas vied with each other in gaudy, colourful bars and restaurants. It was very hot — in the 90s at least — but there was a slight, cooling breeze and Elizabeth felt content and relaxed. The atmosphere seduced her. She passed the Beach Bar Miami and the quaintly named BBC, decided against the Atlas Beach and the Coco Beach and the Mustapha Beach, and found herself stepping down a spiral staircase into the bowels of Jock's Bar — a paradise of plastic fronds, berries and leaves, fake blossoms thick with dust, grime and sand. Behind the counter, a few grubby bottles perched among cards from Blackpool and Scunthorpe.

'Hulloo thair wyatt wommin. Cairn we sairve yee?'

The speaker was a deep-brown walnut of a man, as old as Neptune, with grizzled white hair and a thick Glaswegian accent virtually impossible to understand.

'Jock's mi nom — yerr hoost. Yerr shairly Anglish. Cairn ah hailp?'

'Well, I thought I'd have a bite to eat ...'

'Bairst fish in Aahfrica — grrilled, frayed, stimmed — fraish as morngg."

She sat at a wicker table with a plastic cloth and, indeed, the red snapper was absolutely delicious and the green salad crisp and tasty. A plate of golden chips were fried 'in true Scottish tradition'. Elizabeth was a teetotaller, but allowed Jock to persuade her to sip spritzers — cooling tall glasses combining the best Moroccan white wine, acceptable though apparently flavoured with just a soupçon of petrol, with large quantities of chilled Perrier. After a while, the sipping became gulping. She was not aware that an entire bottle of Gris de Gris had been consumed and another was half empty. To her unaccustomed palate it tasted like mildly interesting fizzy water.

The beach stretched for miles. Black Ethiopians tried to convince her to buy carved animals or woven scarves. Children turned cartwheels in the water. Tourists burned vermillion under the blazing sun, slathering their bodies ineffectually with expensive creams. The sounds of traffic on the road above blended with the shrieking and squealing on the beach. Transistors whined dance music and Arabic tunes. Bathers strolled past her table towards the tiny changing rooms and crude showers — nothing more than tall taps hooked like cranes above drains.

Elizabeth became maudlin.

She remembered a most disturbing and unpleasant lunch with her old friend Kenneth Jenkins, the theatre critic, at Harvey Nichols, on one of her occasional trips to London.

'That's your problem and your talent, darling. You are totally superficial. You've never felt anything deeply in your life. You were cosseted and cared for and left money so you've never suffered or seen life, which enables you to churn out hundreds of comfortable, empty romances with cut-out, cardboard characters and identical, clichéd plots. And, of course, the punters, who are simple souls, love them and buy them in their millions. You're a great success providing pap to the masses. Don't knock it — but don't think you're any better than a simple production line, the literary equivalent of a conveyor belt.'

His wicked, boyish face had crinkled up into that cackling laugh and she had joined in the merriment ... but the barb had hit home.

Here she was, 51 years old, still a virgin, living alone except for the servants, rich as sin yet parsimonious to the core, and nobody of any significance had ever praised her work.

She thought her books were good. Well crafted. Cleverly penned. A sculpture in words. There was humour there, and subtlety. Yet she was considered a mere Mills and Boon spinner of page-turners.

Other, similar, writers like Alan Bennett were regarded as geniuses and taken very seriously as creative artistes. They numbered BBC executives and similar worthy tastemakers amongst their admirers.

But the fact was — the novels of Elizabeth Regina were bought by many more yet considered by the literary establishment as empty froth on a par with Barbara Cartland.

'Oh, come on, Kenneth. Hodder Headline wouldn't publish that sort of garbage. They think I'm a superior novelist. Look at the character of Proctor in Before Dawn. He's a complex hero, muddled and confused, much like Darcy in Pride and Prejudice. I hold that my works are just as noble and deep as the books of Jane Austen.'

'Rubbish, darling. OK, they are not quite as automatic pilot, colour-me-in as Cartland's, but nobody has even given you a decent review — in fact, I challenge you to produce any review at all. Your novels are simply not considered worthy of examination or opinion.'

She had to admit to the truth of that. Two dozen published stories and never a single appearance in The Sunday Times Book Review.

And Jenkins had a point about her lifestyle, too. Safe, cosy, predictable and traditional. She knew that, secretly; that was why she had decided on this holiday. Fate had thrown her the opportunity of two weeks out of character.

A seedy, elderly, grizzled man breathed whisky into her face.

'Jock tells me you're a fellow Brit. Mind if I join you for coffee?'

No, absolutely not, never talk to strangers, never accept invitations, don't allow people to intrude into your space ...

'Why not? Please sit down. My name's Elizabeth. What's yours?'

Two

'*E*dward. Edward Vere. Been here years. Love it, understand it, wouldn't ever dream of going back to Blighty. What's your excuse?'

She laughed. 'I've only just arrived but I do see your point. The sunshine and the atmosphere ... it's so exotic.'

'No, that's where you're wrong. It may be exotic to you but it's simply Tangier when you've lived here a while. And the sunshine gets very irritating — one longs for the storms and the rain. The true Morocco is not for the tourists. It's a way of thinking. An attitude. And one which, when you begin to understand it, can be deeply troubling to the European observer. Almost every value you hold dear needs abandoning and every rooted distrust becomes true. Can't explain it in a minute. Couldn't even do so in a week. Actually, I don't think you'd want to know.'

'You might be right. I'll need a few more hours to decide whether I actually want to know it better. But I've got two weeks ...'

She told him of her life — just enough, not too much. The bare bones but none of the intimacies, though Kenneth, she thought ruefully, would claim she had no intimacies. Then Eddie, as he instructed her to call him, filled in the colours of his own background.

Born of aristocratic stock, taught at a very disreputable pseudo public school and minor university, into the Army like everybody in the 30s ... a pattern of anecdotes and facts rattled out, entertaining, witty, fascinating. Old friends, teachers and parents, life as a teenager in the 20s after the First World War, army training, officer gossip, regulations, affairs, near marriage ending in spiritual divorce, battling the Germans, getting demobbed, thinking of a job, hating the British Establishment, meeting friends on their way to visit friends in Morocco, loving the freedom, coming more frequently to Tangier, buying a bar, losing the bar, making ends meet, reaching 80 ...

His blue eyes sparkled like a man half his age. He was old and experienced with sagging brown wrinkled skin and a shock of white hair, looking like an old soak but talking like a lover, articulate and bright. His hands moved with the telling of the tales, fingers illustrating as they danced in the air. She was hypnotised by the flavour of his soul and mildly intoxicated by the potent, watered down Gris de Gris. He accepted several Scotches as though they were earned, which perhaps they were. They sat and talked until dusk and the beach began to empty, and agreed to meet again the next day to talk further.

Elizabeth wandered back to her hotel and sank on to the soft bed. Her head was throbbing, whether totally due to the alcohol or partly because of the sun and the conversation was unclear. But this was just what she'd been looking for. The real world and somebody prepared to bare their soul and search for hers. If Kenneth was right and she was superficial, then this was the holiday experience she needed.

The following day, she was disappointed to find no Eddie at the beach. She sipped a coffee — no more spritzers, thank you, ever again — and watched the crowd swell. Tiny children charmed then stole belongings from tourists. Hawkers shouted repeated slogans with the automation of drugged zombies. The barbecue smoke spiralled into the air and char-grilled the atmosphere. Then, just as she was about to order lunch on her own, bored by Jock's small talk, a gruff whisper hissed down her neck.

'You start early, don't you? Some of us hardly know it's day until the sun's in the middle of the sky!'

Eddie lowered his bony frame into the spare chair at her table.

'Gonna buy me lunch?'

'Brazen is too good a word for you,' she smiled. 'Is it obligatory or merely customary for men to sponge off women in this town?'

'Well, I look at it this way. You expect me to entertain you. You're new to Morocco, don't speak Arabic and I'm still just British enough, and definitely old enough, for you to feel safe. You can get the sights and sounds of Tangier second-hand, without lifting a foot or a finger. Sitting in Jock's comfortable bar, eating his delicious seafood, you can listen and absorb with no effort whatsoever. Surely that's enough to warrant feeding me?'

'No — brazen is exactly the right word. And yes, I do want to understand this city and why it has won your heart ...'

'Not my heart — just my body,' he interrupted with a twinkle.

'Yai're a roooogue, Veerre,' said Jock, bringing a bottle of whisky to the table. 'Thes'll cost yer, Mrs Regeena, 'nd ah guarrrantee't won't be worrrth it.'

'It's "Ms",' grinned Elizabeth, 'and let me be the judge of that.'

Dull the Scotsman might be, but he did know a fresh fish when he saw one, however it might be pronounced, and the nameless white slab on a bed of lettuce was quite delectable.

Eddie spoke about the way Arabic men treated women, described a Hamman, discussed pederasts, defined the scents of the spices in the casbah, commented on the King and the vast new mosque in Casablanca ('not popular with the people who generously paid for it!') and went on for ages about the state of Moroccan television.

'Everyone exists on satellite dishes here, even the poor middle-class, a section which is growing rapidly. The powers that be don't realise the damage to the culture a diet of MTV and VH1 can be to the young Moroccans. There are McDonald's here now and huge shopping malls. In many ways, it's becoming frighteningly Western and all the charms that tempted me here are slipping away.'

'But there is still that undercurrent of danger?'

'Yes — more thanks to the cross-breeding and immigration of bizarre Brits and Yanks. You should meet Paul Bowles, a strange little creature if ever I saw one ... you've read *The Sheltering Sky*?'

'Of course.'

'Oh, I forgot you were a writer. Very grand. Bloomsbury set or the current equivalent, I expect?'

'Not quite.'

'What then? Agatha Christie? History books? Guide books?'

She smiled.

'Nothing you would ever have read, Eddie, but I do OK.'

'I'll tell you what. Let's go out tonight and I'll take you to one of the joints where all the real characters hang out. That's where you'll get true atmosphere. You'll have to pay, naturally.'

'Naturally.'

Three

*M*aria's was in an alleyway down which no normal, healthy soul would set foot. Teeming with the most doubtful of characters, scarred and mutilated beings with not one set of decent eyes between them, features dented and broken and crooked.

The club itself was not a lot better.

The sole reason for its existence was the owner. A blowzy, jolly, Northern lass gone to seed decades past, she had moved to the city when she married a Moroccan who had then inconveniently died. Fortunately, she had inherited this small café and turned it into a haven for ex-patriots. With the largest breasts Elizabeth had ever seen, she billowed out of her combined Arab and British outfit like an earth mother. When she laughed, she threw her head back and bellowed with deep, rich cackles, guffaws of humour like the crashing waves on a tropical shore.

There were vases full of imitation plastic Oiseaux de Paradis — a spiky flower, all yellow petals and sharp orange beaks. Mats covered in cigarette burns. Cheap mementos from visitors who felt the décor would be improved by them. The inevitable inflated fish bristling poisonously in death. And a collection of elderly European queens, bristling poisonously in wit.

They sat at the corner of the bar ('my spot') and Elizabeth insisted on mineral water to accompany Eddie's treble Scotches.

'Now that,' he announced far too loudly, pointing at an effeminate German in his 70s, sculptured blond hair coiffeured across his bald pate and held in place with several cans of spray, 'is Frau Meisel, once a star of the Kraut TV screen but now propping up this counter after an unfortunate incident back home which we won't go into just yet. Abdul is his boyfriend.'

Abdul was a strapping young Arab with long lashes who looked as though he'd prefer to be elsewhere.

'So happy for to see you, my dear,' said Frau Meisel, simpering. 'Any friend of Eddie's is welcome in this establishment. Wilkommen.'

'And this,' said Vere, gesturing at a quiet, thin man in a corner on his own, 'is our resident celebrity novelist, Venom.'

'Pleased to meet you,' said the recipient of the description, rising to greet Elizabeth. 'And

I'm not, of course, called Venom. As you get to know me better you, too, will start to wonder at the nickname bestowed on me by these sad inebriates. I'm Henry R Hathaway.'

'How do you do?' said Elizabeth, impressed. Henry R Hathaway was a fairly successful writer. His books were few and far between and, when they did come out, were inevitably praised by critics and compared to the works of William Golding. She personally had struggled with a couple, finding them incredibly obtuse and packed with literary innuendo and confusing allegory.

The only reason anybody had heard of him in the world at large was that his most recent novel, *Foundations* had been made into an acclaimed art movie called *Le Roman de Sable*, wittily translated by lovers of Noel Coward as 'Sand Encounter'.

Elizabeth found him intriguing. He was about 40, unprepossessing and ordinary, with soft dark hair, black eyes like polished pebbles and average features.

'You, too, are a writer?' he asked softly.

'Yes, I've had a few books published,' she said and lied, 'I've read your novels with much enjoyment.'

'Thank you so much,' answered Hathaway, his thin lips brushed by the shadow of a smile, before he slipped quietly back into his seat, nursing his beer and watching.

'Why do you call him Venom?' she whispered to Eddie who answered, rather too loudly, she felt.

'Oh, he's a poisonous snake. Seems polite and soft spoken until he gets a couple of drinks inside him. Then the tongue slides out and closely resembles a razor blade. You'll find out. Just wait ... watch and listen.'

'What are you doing here, love?' asked Maria. 'Holiday?'

'Yes, taking in the sunshine, relaxing, getting a tan I hope, experiencing local culture ...'

Maria giggled. 'Then Eddie's not the man for you, dear. He thinks CULTURE is a brand of gin!'

She was instantly open, friendly.

'I think you could do better than that glass of water,' she said. 'Now I concoct a delicious and refreshing libation called the Strangled Chicken. No alcohol. Not sweet. Salty yet thirst quenching. Wanna try?'

'Why not?'

As she mixed the ingredients, Maria gave a running commentary.

'She's splashing Worcestershire Sauce into the huge glass. Seven ice cubes. Like it spicy, dear? Not too spicy? Then she'll forgo the tabasco. Celery salt. Garlic salt. Gallons of Clamato Juice, the finest nectar ever created by man, combining tomatos and clam juice. It has to be flown in by the crate specially. Now here she adds the secret ingredient.'

Mugging like a villain in a bad silent movie, she removed a bottle from the fridge. It contained a cloudy liquid, which she poured dramatically into the glass.

'She adds the sprig of mint for colour and contrast and *voilà* — your individual Strangled Chicken. We do a more lethal version with white rum called a Poisoned Chicken, too, if you ever feel brave.'

Elizabeth sipped it cautiously. It was delicious.

'What's the secret ingredient?' she asked.

'That's a secret,' laughed Maria. 'No, it's simply boiled-down fresh chicken stock, well chilled and filtered through muslin to extract the fat and bits. My variation of Bloody Bullshot or Virgin Bullshot in your case,' she said.

'It's very bad for you,' a voice hissed in her ear. Hathaway had slipped out of his seat and sidled on to the stool beside her. 'Packed with monosodium glutamate. Killer.'

'See what I mean,' Eddie whispered in the other. 'Now watch him start destroying everybody's reputation.'

'One more of your lagers please, Maria,' ordered Venom politely.

On closer inspection, Elizabeth noticed he had extraordinarily bad skin. It was lumpy, as though porridge had been inserted through the pores. Probably the result of teenage acne. His breath smelt foul, too. But he remained silent.

'Are you liking the sunshine and culture of Tangier?' asked Frau Meisel.

'I've only just got here but so far it's terrific,' she replied with a smile.

Frau Meisel cuddled Abdul who looked decidedly uncomfortable.

'You must prepare to enjoy the fruits of the city,' leered the German.

'Vile queen,' hissed Venom, gesturing for another beer. 'In Germany, she was the subject of an appalling scandal involving young boys. Even here she is only just tolerated. I could tell you stories you would not believe ...'

'No, thank you,' said Elizabeth rather frostily.

At this moment the door burst open and an extraordinary creature staggered in. Supported by a pair of crutches much too tall for his tiny body, the dwarf was one of the ugliest creatures Elizabeth had ever seen. Well, he wasn't a dwarf in fact — just under 5ft but twisted out of shape, he was clearly part-Arab and part-European — long, bulbous nose, sneering mouth, straggly moustache, receding hair, black and greasy. The energy and concentration needed to propel himself caused his lips to grimace and drool.

'Ah, our resident freak,' Eddie declared. 'Elizabeth — this is Kirk. English mother who passed away the moment she saw him, and who can blame her? We're rather proud of Kirk. Not many communities can boast a gay, crippled, half-caste amongst them. Come and be bought a drink, mate.'

The little man lurched towards them and amazingly perched on a stool without losing grip of either crutch, looking like a gargoyle squatting on a pin.

'Kirk Kurabbi, at your service. Pay no attention to the loud-mouthed comments of your elderly friend. He's just jealous of my youth and beauty.'

He threw his head back and pealed with laughter and, indeed, he was both young and beautiful when his face erupted like that. His dark-brown eyes sparkled. His misshapen features puckered in fun, showing perfect white teeth. The transformation from toad to prince was instant.

'So what brings you to Maria's? Yet another sad seduction of an innocent tourist by that raddled old hetero?'

'You could put it that way — but it's been merely an intellectual rape. We met at Jock's Beach and he persuaded me to come here and discover the richer side of Tangerine life.'

'Richer? You'll be poorer after several of Maria's overcharged drinks on your bill. So who have you met?'

'Only you so far,' interposed Eddie, 'unless you count Frau Meisel, Abdul and Venom! Nobody else does. We just arrived. What's your poison?'

As the evening progressed, a selection of ex-patriots or, as in Kirk's instance, their offspring, wandered into the restaurant. Elizabeth treated her two companions to Maria's *Raie au Beurre Noir*, the speciality of the house and surprisingly good, too, though Elizabeth was beginning to wonder if you could ever eat anything other than fish in Tangier. The air was dense with smoke and the fumes of cooking — without air-conditioning, it was boiling hot, although she'd noticed that the nights grew very cool.

Amused by how out of place the new arrival looked, Maria had wiped her hands on a tea cloth, left bar duties to a handsome young Arab (rumoured to be poking her frequently with an enormous penis, though none of the queens had dared get close enough to examine it) and joined the threesome at their table in the eating area.

She'd been a friend of Kirk's mother in Yorkshire. The two of them had come to Tangier on holiday — like so many of the ex-patriots — and fallen in love with two Arabs. Both were students and penniless, no catch even for ambitious Moroccans, but love crossed the most mercenary barriers ...

Elizabeth felt herself drifting into novel mode ...

Hungrily, the strong Arab pulled young Maria into his arms. His urges were irresistible, his lusts unquenchable. He tore at her bodice (did girls really ever have bodices?) and ripped her silken shirt apart, revealing delicious white melons of British bosoms ... months later, living together in poverty, the kind of basic squalor a Yorkshire girl could never have imagined, they were still blissfully happy ... Meanwhile, her friend and his cousin were equally in love ... the weddings were a traditional Islamic ceremony ... their families came, scowling displeasure and predicting dire consequences, the misery of being a woman in a Muslim world ... but then her friend gave birth to a monster and died in the effort ... her husband was inconsolable and took to drink (not a polite Muslim habit) ... Maria determined to look after the boy as if he were her own ... her husband's father died and left him the small café ... then, suddenly, her beloved died too, shortly to be followed by the inebriated father of poor, ugly Kirk ... so they were alone, the widow and the child, struggling to cope in a cruel world ... her English family urged her to return but, by then, Tangier was her home and her few years of memories were very happy ones ...

Twenty-five years later, Maria was in her 50s and Kirk was a man, if you could call the strange, deformed creature by that name.

Yet he fascinated Elizabeth. His energy and anger at the world were phenomenal. Most of his loathing he reserved for the British Government who, for some strange bureaucratic reason, would not grant him citizenship. His knowledge of all things British was vast, through talking to Brits and reading the imported papers from cover to cover. He did very little work, though he would sometimes manage to persuade a lonely old tourist homosexual that the ultimate indignity — being fucked by a crippled dwarf — might be exotic and erotic and would certainly require sums of money.

He chattered openly about himself. He was extremely fit, once you discounted the deformities, and had a keen brain and ready sense of humour ... 'When it comes to Sex Abuse, it's not the sex that's wrong, it's the abuse.' He gave as good as he took when the ex-patriots goaded him, which they did fondly, because they saw him as their mascot ... 'They only live here because nobody wants them, which makes them the same as me really.' He adored Maria and she obviously felt the same way about him ... 'She's fat and ugly and 100 times more attractive than me.' Maria talked extensively about how the city had changed from the late 1960s to the present day.

As Elizabeth tucked herself into her luxurious El Minzah bed that night, many pounds sterling lighter, she reflected on the humanity in these bizarre people. And it was then that the idea came to her.

She would write that 'significant' work, based on Kirk and the crowd around him. Rather than turn Maria's story into yet another Regina novel, she would explore the extraordinary twists and turns of fate that had created Kirk and his situation.

All life is written here. From the real-life experiences, a truly worthy, deep, critically acclaimed tale could be woven.

That would show Kenneth Jenkins what for.

Four

I speak English and I speak Arabic and I speak French.

There are many Chairmen of international corporations who cannot boast that. There are doctors and scientists and artistes and stars who can only just muster their own language, let alone anybody elses. Yet I am virtually imprisoned in a tiny Third World country, locked away from travel outside, banned from even visiting the home of my mother.

Small wonder, then, that I am bitter.

But add to that my birthright. Stunted, crippled, orphaned, ugly, short and gay.

It's enough to make an angel cry. And I'm no angel.

I've stolen from European pockets whilst cramming my weapon up their anuses. I've taken bags from shoulders in the crowded *medina*. I've buggered under-age boys and I've sold drugs to tourists.

And that's just in one day.

But through it all, I've retained my sense of humour. I cackle at the world whilst ripping it off. I chortle with glee at my own misfortunes. After all, you've got to laugh.

When I was very young, I learned how to please the queens. Rub them, suck them, fondle them, feel them, kiss them.

It didn't matter that I was a hideous little sod. I was well endowed and technically innocent — that was all they wanted, dropping by our shores in search of thrills, the thrills denied them in their 1970s and 1980s post-Victorian land of anally-retentive morality.

Hypocrisy, smugness, class systems, the dying Empire.

Sometimes I wondered how they'd react if I dropped by to visit them in their ancestral mansions. Many had wives and children securely locked away. I'd arrive for tea, easing myself out of the black taxi in a tangle of wooden sticks and paralysed limbs. Horror on their faces. Oh, I was fine millions of miles and a hundred cultures away — never any danger of my infecting their polite society. But even though they returned from the airport and fondly pecked their spouses and offspring on the cheeks whilst my sperm was sloshing about inside the cheeks of their bottoms, the thought of my twisted features snarling at their acceptable appendages would have caused their hearts to stop.

Which is probably why I'd never have done it. Full of bile I might be, but it is a non-destructive, affectionate kind of fury.

They had given me money, after all, and, in their sadly limited way, love. They had provided me with a superficial way to reach orgasm. Why ruin their lives for a joke? My whole life was a joke already. That was quite enough.

It's not much of an existence coping in Tangier. There are the basic costs and expenditures, like paying off the corrupt police officers. Those constant bouts of harrassment from bloated coppers with giant bellies — the more immoral, the larger the stomachs — every one of whom have pock-marked skin, bad breath, bullet heads and lousy teeth. Blackmailers and extortionists. They know they can terrify the pederasts with threats and ominous hints and they think they can get money from me by hinting at long prison sentences in the worst gaols. And I have to help Maria make ends meet. I am not speaking literally, of course; I have far too much respect for my adopted mother for that, thank you. There is the learning and the consumption of information (though most of the international newspapers are free, donated after reading by the tourists) as well as the clothes to cover this deformed body and keep the passers-by from having the frightful shock of seeing me naked.

Once, I tried to smuggle myself on to the car ferry crossing to Algeciras. I just couldn't stand the confinement any longer. I'd have coped with the Spanish immigration officials at the other end and dodged through the controls, but I never even got on board ship. Not exactly mobile, you see.

Maria would have missed me dreadfully and I do have many friends in Tangier, though most would never admit it publicly. Fondness is better shared with barbs and witticisms, sneers and criticisms. The genuine kindness is always there, though, concealed beneath the surface. Still, I'd sacrifice it all for the chance of seeing Yorkshire.

I can feel it in my poor misshapen bones. The rolling, misty, green meadows. The sheep. The cloth caps. The beer. The soft accents. I've seen the photos and heard the stories.

That's where my mother spent her youth and there's a strong, urgent pull on my soul. I know, I'm half-Moroccan; more than half, since I've spent so many years here. And my relatives here treat me well, which is more than I can say for the total disinterest — nay, silence — emanating from the hills and vales of England. But it simply seems so unfair.

The answer is to sweeten the sour by making millions here and then buying my way back. But it's not as easy as it sounds, despite the fact that

I'm astute, intelligent and a speedy learner. There just aren't the facilities for a gay, crippled half-caste that there ought to be. You'd think there would be good fairies hanging from the rafters, desperate to sprinkle magic dust over my pathetic, deformed anatomy. A benefactor bursting to save my soul and to drag me away from all this. A missionary laden with the zealot's desire to save my soul in return for a blow job. But it is not to be. Such *dénouements* are merely for the chapters of fiction and this is beastly reality over here.

So I potter along, making the best of things, trying not to turn nasty. And every day I get older and arguably uglier (though many would decree that impossible), and the chance seems to become even more blurred and distant.

Meantime, this is my story. It's brief enough to interest you for a few hours. Pick it up and put it down. While away the odd bored moment. It's varied and packed with pathos. There's even a trifle of romance and a pinch of drama contained in its pages. But a word of caution. Don't feel pity or shed tears. Don't light the fires of charity because they mean nothing to me and they simply diminish my dignity. I urge you not to dig too deep or to see too much. But from the simplest tale come a thousand lessons if you are prepared to learn them. As the poet once said — keep an open mind; let it all hang out.

Five

'Would you mind if I write a novel based on your life and experiences?'

Elizabeth had decided on the direct approach and Kirk's reaction was delight.

'Of course I wouldn't mind. I'd be very flattered. But are you sure your readers are ready for me? They sound like rather a placid, contented lot.'

It was a fair point and Elizabeth had already considered it.

'I don't think I'll publish it under my own name. For a start, I want it to stand or fall in its own right. Secondly, I don't want the preconceptions so closely associated with my name to dictate the kind of attention it would get. So I'll publish it under a pseudonym. Of course, that will probably mean nobody will read it. It would be judged as a first novel and they are notoriously ignored by the critics and public alike. But it will have the chance to exist as a separate entity. It won't just be your life story. It will absorb observations and have a plot unconnected with reality, but I'd like to trawl through your history and pick your brains.'

'Fine by me, but I must warn you where I keep them!'

And they roared with laughter at his implication.

They were strolling through the narrow, muddy streets of the *medina*. Last night, there had been one of the extraordinary, torrential, tropical rain storms that lasted for ten minutes and totally failed to cool the atmosphere, yet drenched the earth and turned the roads into slippery rivers of slime. Progress with Kirk was slow at the best of times. Churning his distorted body and waving his flaccid legs about as his strong arms pivoted the crutches, contorting his movement like a crippled snake, he weaved sideways and backwards almost as much as forwards, yet somehow he still managed eventually to move in the direction intended.

Anybody watching him must have been reminded of Dickens' Quilp from *The Old Curiosity Shop* — an Arab version, darker, more evil, snarling, spitting, dribbling and frothing in his attempts to make his uncontrollable limbs function. But Elizabeth had already discovered how far from the truth the superficial impression was. This was an intelligent man, soured by bad luck but not pessimistic, powered by humour and observation.

The urchins avoided pestering her for money, seeing her companion. Even though she looked like the typical Western tourist, neat and smart except for the splattering of mud on her stockings, impeccably dressed in a tidy blue suit, hair in perfect shape, broad in the beam but smooth skinned, they realised that she was protected. She'd crossed the line between visitor and native. Her mascot was so well known in Tangier that any friend of his demanded respect. So there were no requests to guide her around or show her the sights or begging pleas on behalf of terminal relatives.

The slow progress and lack of interruption enabled her to take in the flavour of Tangier and, with it, Morocco. The tastes and odours which dominated — cinnamon, herbs, burnt meat, coffee, tanned leather, drains — all blending, yet distinctive. The high, irritating transistor blare of music, shrill and harsh, mimicking the sound of the *muezzins* and their call to prayer. The hysterical, energetic rush of children pounding past, grabbing each other and chirping with laughter. Poor they might be in material goods, but endowed with vast quantities of the joys of existence.

'Keep away from him, my friend,' Venom had hissed at her during a drunken moment in

Maria's bar. 'He's dangerous. Only after your money. Wants a passport. Will never tell you about the awful things he's done. Worse than you could ever imagine. Cancer for your soul. Avoid at all costs. Avoid.'

Kirk lived in a room above a friend's shop — a meagre, bare place but clean enough, with basic facilities. It was in one of the approach roads to the casbah. Downstairs, a jumble of objects tempted the passing Moroccan. Cheap transistors, pirated tapes, cameras, pots and pans, patterned clay bowls for couscous and *tagine*, electric cooking rings at low prices without basic safety precautions. They talked there for hour after hour — Elizabeth taking copious notes. They spent the days on Jock's Beach and the evenings in Maria's. After a while, she felt she knew the taste of the various fish dishes intimately before she even sampled them.

He spoke of his hopes, dreams, fears and joys. He analysed the culture and explained the customs. He spoke perfect English, of course — Maria had seen to that — and fluent French. Elizabeth soon got to know several of Kirk and Eddie's other friends — mostly queens who had moved to the city when their predilections were still unacceptable in Europe and had grown too fond of the place to leave when civilisation changed. As a result, they tended to be over 60 and blended their humour with acid, sometimes forgetting the humour altogether.

Many knew Paul Bowles and the literary set. Some had even met Joe Orton on his legendary trips. They were universally shockingly irreligious, which didn't appear to offend their Muslim acquaintances at all. Several smoked dope — or *kif* as it was known — with impunity. They all received regular care packages from England containing vital, unavailable essentials like Earl Grey Tea, Bovril, Marmite and Worchestershire Sauce.

Kirk became pleasantly attached to Elizabeth. He'd expected a job, some money, a few hours providing her with colour before she returned to Britain and he forgot her. He'd known enough tourist relationships to be aware that the friendships paled as the sunshine reverted to the chill of English weather. Protestations of undying love rapidly became affectionate postcards and then terminal silence. So he was quite prepared for this superficially enjoyable encounter to drift into history. But the more they talked, the better he liked her.

She was so perceptive and intelligent. He'd never known anybody observe so much detail, but she could glimpse beneath the surface, too. Every native idiosyncrasy added to her understanding. He introduced her to families he'd never normally allow to mix with a European and she charmed them, too. The standard assumption of future financial benefit disappeared shortly after they met her and dissolved into genuine affection.

And she brought out the best in him. He'd never been treated as a normal human being by a tourist before. It made him think differently, behave naturally, even reconsider his own attitudes and beliefs.

She, on the other hand, had surprised herself by the depth of her feelings for him. Not only did he fascinate her with the story of his roots and his development, but he stirred her human interest by showing a real intelligence. His education had been basic but his natural curiosity had taught him more skills than anyone she'd ever known. Not just the art of survival and the technical powers of language and communication, but the thirst for information. Just as she observed, he consumed facts and opinions with a ravaging appetite.

One day, as a treat, Elizabeth took Kirk for lunch at the restaurant in her hotel. It was beautiful, tables laid out in the cool courtyard and quite mouth-watering cuisine. Kirk behaved very well and, afterwards, they went upstairs to her room to continue her interview. She helped him lie on the bed, though normally he disdained any physical assistance. Suddenly, tangled up together, she felt his arms strengthen around her and he pulled her on top of him. Half-laughing nervously, she remonstrated but he was enormously strong. She felt herself pinned face down, nearly stifling in the pillow.

His hands were scrabbling at her underwear and then she knew the worst pain she had ever experienced as he entered her from behind. It was as though a red-hot poker were being stuffed inside her — ruthless, violent, agonising yet also, in a bizarre way, erotic.

As he pumped brutally inside her, she felt a fountain build up on the other side, as though she was going to have to pee. Then he climaxed, with a heave and a push that virtually split her open and, as he did so, she felt the most incredible sensation of electricity and shuddering running through her own body. She realised that, for the first time in her life, she had come.

He pulled away and she froze in embarrassment, aware of the wet patch between her legs.

'Well, that was a first for me,' he said. 'How was it for you? As good as getting it the normal way?'

'I've never had it any way,' she gasped, sounding as though the air was being squeezed out of her lungs through a miniature valve.

'You're joking. That was your first time for anything? No wonder you're so starched.'

'It just never came along.'

He laughed. 'That's one way of putting it.'

She turned over.

'You'd better fix your face,' he chuckled. 'Your make-up is so smudged you look like a

Jonathan King

female version of me!'

'I don't think you should have done that,' she swallowed.

'You're probably right. Still, life is full of doing things you shouldn't. *Je ne regrette rien.* Anyway, you should be proud to have awakened the tiniest flicker of heterosexuality in me!'

'Was that what it was?'

'Yes ... I think so, plus fondness and affection. I enjoyed it, actually. You still haven't told me if you did.'

'I think I did, as it happens, though every fibre of my body was telling me I ought not to. You were a bit brutal, weren't you?'

'Sorry about that, but I just got turned on. I've learned to give in to these animal impulses. Resisting them just leads to trouble. And you must remember, I've been sexually active for almost as long as I've been breathing.'

'Yet you've never made love to a woman before?'

'No ... I never could find the desire. So kindly be flattered and go and repair the damage to your melting features!'

This was definitely not the comfy romance normally to be discovered between the pages of an Elizabeth Regina bestseller, she thought as she spent some time in the bathroom. But 51 was getting on a bit and, if she'd determined to seek adventure, this was shaping up nicely to be a cracker.

Six

*E*lizabeth had found a second-hand Apple Mac PowerBook Duo 270c — clearly once the property of a tourist — in a shop near the hotel. It seemed to be in perfect working order, although the spell-check facility, drawing upon American words, was decidedly suspect. Since she had intentionally not brought her own lap-top with her on holiday — having vowed not to write a single word for two weeks — this was an important investment.

'Normally, I dedicate myself to 2,000 words a day when I'm working,' she explained. 'It's a discipline. But I've got exactly ten days left before I return to England with a completed offering. That's 100,000 words. So I've got to do 10,000 a day.'

'Ah, but inspiration is so much easier than discipline,' smiled Kirk.

And inspired she was. Quite happy for Kirk

and Eddie to be there, she hammered out a few thousand at the beach, a few more in Maria's at night and several thousand early in the morning, rising as the sun did, putting five hours of effort into the computer before anyone saw her. Steaming mugs of coffee kept her going (the tea tasted dreadful with the odd Moroccan milk, but the coffee appeared unaffected), sweetened with lashings of honey. Kirk and Eddie were amused that she seemed quite capable of composing whilst continuing to participate in their conversations.

She made no notes, had no plot or plan on paper. In her head she could feel it was right and her fingers did the talking.

Every now and then, she'd look up and ask Kirk a question.

'If you inherited a fortune, what would you do with it?'

'Try to ease the suffering of people born like me.'

'Even before rectifying your own problems?'

'Oh, I'm past rectifying, darling — and, anyway, I've become quite fond of this body. I wouldn't know how to walk if I looked like you lot!'

Hilarity from the assembled ex-pats whilst Elizabeth went back to her frenzied typing.

Other tourists swam or bronzed or read three-day-old newspapers but Elizabeth tapped on the keys, correcting as she went, adding spaces, checking the word count, rephrasing and editing, happy in her hobby. Eddie would rattle out a commentary on the history and behaviour of German families, Spanish fairies, Italian stallions, Russian explorers, embroidering imaginary backgrounds and tales. Kirk would add extra, frequently distressing, levels of fantasy and imagination. The three of them would invent names and stories to fit the holidaying hundreds. Yet still Elizabeth worked on, the words seeming to flow unhindered from her soul, whilst her mind, eyes and body were otherwise occupied.

At nights, Kirk occasionally came back to her hotel and several times they made love, only more gently and affectionately now, but always from behind because, as Kirk said, 'I can't do it any other way!'

It was clear that he really cared for her. He often did unexpected, romantic things, like sending flowers to her hotel first thing in the morning. They were delivered with breakfast; enormous vases overflowing with roses and more exotic blooms. She asked him whether he was just trying to get an English woman to ease his entry into Great Britain.

'It didn't do much for my dad or Maria's man, did it?' he replied.

'Well, at least there's no danger of my getting pregnant,' said Elizabeth, which made him laugh so much he almost fell over.

She was amazed by how easily the words came. Unlike her previous novels, which were like pulling teeth (when did they last pull teeth?), this was like breathing. She switched on the PC and the screen lit up. For a moment she looked at it and then, not waiting for that dreadful moment, she started automatically. Tens, hundreds, thousands of sentences flew through the wires and bytes. From Kirk's experience and her own observations she tapped into the fountain of art.

'What will you call it?' he asked.

'Ramadan Mislaid,' she said. 'It was something you came up with when I was asking whether you observed the traditions of Islam ... "It all somehow passed me by," you said, "Allah got lost and Ramadan mislaid." I liked the sound of that.'

'Let's hope you don't have a *fatwah* put on you,' he said.

If she needed reference books, Eddie Vere had several libraries collected in his rooms. Mind you, he had to find what she needed as only he could understand the chaotic filing system but the speed of his delivery was far better than any civic facility. He'd scurry around like a bronzed beetle, scuttling back seconds later bearing dusty, out-of-print volumes containing exactly the information she needed. She once asked him how he'd acquired so many books, and discovered that he'd inherited many from an old friend who had passed away, and kept enlarging it with tomes imported by visiting tourists.

Kirk, Eddie, Maria and Jock had adopted her into their clique. She had her own seat reserved at the bar counter and a fish special had been christened Elizabeth's Squid (not the most attractive of sea creatures to bear her name, perhaps). They thought of her as one of them. Considering that a week ago she'd been a typical Surrey woman, successfully churning out pop pap and never allowing a grain of doubt to enter into her daily philosophy, that was quite an achievement.

Every now and then, Henry R Hathaway approached her. He wasn't sure what she was doing or why she was so fascinated by the Maria Mafia, as he sourly called them, but he'd seen her pummelling away on the keyboard of her Apple Mac. Was she a writer, too, he wondered? Kind of, she answered, warned by Eddie never to say too much. Would she mind him using her in a book he was writing? Not at all, she'd chuckled, amused by the irony. Did she really care about these dreadful people or was she just using them, like he was? No, they were her friends. Would she like to visit the genuine Tangerines, not the ghastly peasants associated with that cripple? Another time, she thanked him. Surely they must have mutual friends in the publishing worlds of London or New York? He had small homes everywhere, he boasted.

Perhaps they could meet up for afternoon tea in a more civilised town and laugh about the absurd antics of these strange types? Perhaps.

Venom was tolerated but not liked. They accepted his drinks and allowed him to watch from a distance and cast barbs, but they kept him at arm's length. Even Frau Meisel was more highly regarded because he lived there, warts and all. He was a reject from Western society whereas Venom merely dipped into their waters like an elderly dowager testing a cesspool with the toe of a wrinkled foot. It amused her to see them clam up when he was within earshot. Nobody else would have noticed the instant change in their conversation and attitude but the shutters came down and they concealed every important facet of their lives and thoughts automatically.

He'd grilled everyone. Who was she? Why was she typing all the time? And he'd tried to spread poison. She was a tabloid journalist, out to expose important visitors. She was using them. She'd told him of her vilest intentions. They ignored him.

Neither complicated nor sophisticated, they nevertheless could sense the genuine when it appeared. Elizabeth was genuine; Venom was not.

When the time came for Henry R Hathaway to take his leave, he simply disappeared. No farewells. One day there, the next day not.

Someone had seen him at the airport, sneaking through immigration control. He'd be back. Unfortunately. Meanwhile, it concerned Elizabeth not at all. She was busily banging away at the keyboard, capturing the atmosphere, interpreting the vibrations, developing the plot.

Kenneth Jenkins had a lot to answer for. And it had only been a passing remark, a casual barb tossed into polite conversation between the Harvey Nick's low-priced but delicious salmon fishcakes and their traditionally respected and very expensive bread and butter pudding.

One night, in bed after having sex, she said ...

'By the way — I don't expect you to give up boys or men. I don't want to change you — just to enjoy you.'

'Oh, but you have changed me,' he replied. 'I'll never be the same again. At the moment, I don't want a boy or a man. If I find myself getting fidgety, I'll tell you, don't worry. I may not be many things but I am painfully honest and open. It simplifies things.'

'Let's agree to keep it that way — both of us. Up-front, everything spoken, no secrets or resentments or hidden doubts or subtle fears. Total integrity no matter what we're feeling — we'll say it to each other. That way this might last.'

'It can't last that long. Don't forget, you're only here for a few more days.'

'We don't have to be with each other for it to

last. There are phones and letters and planes ...
and ferries.'

Kirk laughed again. He was always most
amused when he was the butt of the humour.

Seven

'*H*ere they come! What a pair! Like ze Queen Mother and her pit bull terrier!'

Ludwig Meisel was no terrific Teutonic wit but he had a shared viewpoint. Despite the fact that he, with his numerous jowls, painted features cracking in chemical make-up, hideously-dyed hair tortured beyond belief, saggy, enormous stomach, thin white legs and liver-spotted hands, was not the appropriate companion for handsome, young Abdul, their relationship was time-honoured and natural in Tangier. Most of the town thought Elizabeth and Kirk an ill-matched couple. Somehow, a hideous dwarf and a beautiful girl would have appeared romantic, and an elderly man with vivacious concubine obvious, but this bizarre partnership unsettled the most liberal observer.

It didn't bother them in the least. Elizabeth

continued to dress smartly, cultured pearls coiled round her neck, Marks and Spencer fashions neatly pressed, hair perfectly in place. Kirk would always be the same scruffy, grubby gypsy they had known since his childhood.

Maria seemed unperturbed by the clearly intensifying relationship. She'd decided she liked Elizabeth and, after a succession of totally unsuitable admirers for her adopted son, felt any decent friendship should be cherished, no matter how different the ages.

Edward Vere had felt a slight twinge of jealousy when his budding acquaintance was so firmly taken over but, since Elizabeth had no hesitation in continuing to purchase him vast amounts of liquid and solid refreshment, as well as making it clear that she enjoyed his friendship just as much, if in a different way, he swiftly accepted the inevitable and even congratulated himself on initiating the situation.

But the wider range of Tangier opinion definitely disapproved. There were too many uncomfortable elements even for this most open-minded and tolerant of societies.

And Elizabeth felt the disapproval most keenly in the El Minzah Hotel. Dining couples, so bored with each other's company that they rarely spoke, scowled in open contempt. What on earth was that nice English lady doing with that vile Arab? And he, surely, was simply after her money. Couldn't she see that? Was she so blind as to imagine that he could genuinely desire her plump, middle-aged body?

But the staff were the worst of all. Openly scornful, they virtually spat when Kirk staggered in. There was little they could do. Madam had a suite and Madam could entertain whom she chose. But if she was looking for pleasant Tangerine company, they each had many finer specimens of Arab masculinity to offer from amongst their immediate families.

Oblivious to all this, Ms Regina continued to ask questions and elicit opinions as she pattered away on the key pads and filled the memory chip with stylish prose.

And many of the snooty observers, unknown to themselves, were being carved in the marble of fiction, destined to last much longer on the printed page than they ever would in mere mortality.

The days passed by and, one morning, Elizabeth announced at Jock's Beach that the novel was completed. Printing facilities were too limited to give out hard copies but Kirk and Eddie sneaked a look at the 270c colour screen — replete with blue, brown and green teddy bear motif — and approved of the sections. Elizabeth read out loud certain possibly controversial pieces (she'd already cleared the most sensitive passages privately with Kirk, who had only requested factual corrections) and made them guess the component characters described in certain places, which caused much hilarity.

She herself was impressed by what she'd accomplished. The style and language were totally different from anything she'd ever written before, yet she recognised the technique and construction as her own. Years of training had enabled her to master the grind of bashing out those paragraphs in near-automatic pilot mode. As a result, she was now able to think more closely about characterisation, plot and sub-text. The novel flowed rapidly. The colours were bright. It was predominantly based on Kirk Kurabbi's life, but numerous foreign strands had been inspired and woven into the basic skeleton. It was funny — indeed, there were sequences of near farce, many constructed from Kirk's actual experiences. It was dirty — there were adjectives never before featured in an Elizabeth Regina work. But this was a different Elizabeth Regina.

'What name are you going to use?' Eddie queried.

'How about Leslie Prince?' asked Elizabeth. 'The shortened form of Elizabeth is Liz and Leslie comes close to that, as well as containing a gender ambiguity. Prince is, of course, a royal person and Regina is Latin for Queen, which is why I chose it in the first place.'

'So Regina is not your real name?' asked Kirk, amazed.

'No, that's a pseudonym, too. Elizabeth is the name I was christened with though,' she smiled.

'Well, I'm relieved that I'm dating a queen. *Plus ça change ...*' he said.

For the rest of the day and most of that night, they tried to prise her real surname out of her, something she steadfastly refused to reveal.

Sadly, of course, the completion of the project also marked the end of Elizabeth's holiday. Kirk appeared to take this rather more stoically than Maria or Eddie, both of whom had started to regard Elizabeth as a crucial ingredient in their lives. She was virtually the same age as Maria and the two of them had spent many happy and nostalgic hours discussing details of early television shows and stars, past events, sweet treats from schooldays in the 1950s, shared idols and crushes, the works of Cliff Richard compared to the films of Elvis Presley, fashion peculiarities and the ancient North–South divide (North being north of Watford, of course).

Edward Vere had discovered mutual near-acquaintances — mainly involving the children of his old friends who had grown up and become sterling members of Elizabeth's social scene. He was intrigued by the changes and alterations in British life. He did manage to return to the United Kingdom every year, usually at Christmas, but he found, like many ex-patriots, that memories of the country as it used to be were much more potent and affecting than the ugly reality.

Kirk explained that he'd gone into this with his eyes wide open, was well aware that the relationship would probably finish or at least dwindle as the fortnight passed, cherished it as a valuable and thoroughly enjoyable experience, and now intended to get on with his life which, itself, was by definition more complicated than that of most fully mobile people.

'No regrets at all. A friendship for life, please. Don't consider it a commitment to keep in touch. Only do it if you want to do it. On no account regard me as a charity case. No care packages or favours. Simply behave as you feel inside you want to behave.'

They spent a glorious last night together. In bed, Kirk was as able-bodied as any other man, and much more affectionate. Elizabeth found him surprisingly gentle after their first, alarming encounter. He liked to cuddle and caress — indeed, he seemed to stroke her automatically, even when he was asleep. Since she'd never slept with a man before, she wondered whether they all behaved like this. She suspected not.

As the team assembled at the Moroccan immigration desk at the airport, bidding her a fond farewell, Kirk asked for one last time ...

'Come on. Tell us your real name!'

Since her passport was in her hand and they had been courteous enough not to snatch it, she blushed and admitted it to be Smith.

Part 2

Eight

The flight was one of those horrendously overbooked experiences. Hundreds of Moroccans had decided to bring most of Tangier and parts of Casablanca, Rabat, Marrakech and Fez on board as well, mostly packed in newspapers and wicker baskets. She was surprised not to see chickens or grandparents amongst the pots and stuffed camels.

Elizabeth had pulled rank on the public relations people at Heathrow and had been upgraded to Club Class both ways. She was amused by a French couple attempting to gather their children into place by wheedling, cajoling and pulling childlike faces. They had no idea how ridiculous they looked.

Tourist students, loaded with backpacks so heavy that they would have sunk a ship, bounded up the aisles and somehow crammed their enormous luggage into miniature overhead storage spaces.

GB Airways had decided, in their wisdom that curried chicken would benefit the digestive tracts of their passengers. Elizabeth disagreed.

She sipped an iced orange juice, made final corrections to her 70,000 golden words (fewer than intended but just what the subject needed) and wondered how it would go down with the only person that mattered — her agent.

Years ago, a young Elizabeth Smith had fervent literary ambitions. She'd adored the Brontës and wanted to create works of fiction with as much depth and passion as they had achieved. Her teenage scribbles had dominated the Roedean school magazine. It was her only area of excellence. 'Whatever you may say about Liz,' her classmates said, and it wasn't much, 'she can write.'

Write she could. To order. Miss Deadline, she was fondly called by the staff at the *Guardian* when she moved from secretary to sub-editor to contributor. Not inspired, never original, hardly brilliant but always on time.

Her first novels were rejected rapidly until she was introduced at a book launch in a seamy Fleet Street bar to a tall, skinny, ambitious lady. The room was at least packed. Philip Borman, the scribbler, had made enough friends galore during his adequate career to drag minor celebrities into the restaurant for curling canapés and warm Asti Spumante. His work of art had disappeared without trace but the event had allowed Elizabeth to strike up a mutually amusing bond. She sent her latest manuscript, lovingly bound and typed in single space, to the impressive junior agent. It was returned with the comment, 'virtually unreadable ... double space in future, please ... come and see me', scribbled on the cover.

They had gone for tea to Harvey Nicks — where else? — and, bluntly, the experienced and ambitious agent had told the frustrated and eager naïve writer that her attempts at great art were ridiculous but that her romantic instincts read well.

'More of the love and desire; less of the meaningful insight, darling.'

So Elizabeth had tried again. And the rest was history. Millions of novels sold; fortunes earned; huge acclaim from the specialist audience; hundreds of thousands of devoted fans. What more could a girl, or an agent, ask?

It was therefore with trepidation that Elizabeth surrendered her manuscript via messenger with a simple note ... 'you're not going to like this, but read it anyway.'

'It's brilliant, Elizabeth. The best you've ever done. But I still can't understand why you won't put it out under your own name?'

Lisa Littlejohn was known as Lisa the Teaser in the publishing world. She was one of the finest literary agents in London, employed by the old established firm of A P Watt, and she had represented Elizabeth from the start. An angular, elegant blonde, several years older than she looked, she was never seen out of her twin sets. Indeed, some suspected she slept in them. Round, gold-rimmed spectacles perched on the end of her nose, she could have been your favourite but strict literature teacher at Roedean. Piled on her desk were hundreds of manuscripts, most of which would never be read by anybody else. Elizabeth often wondered where Lisa found the time to read them all. The hopes and dreams of so many talentless yet convinced artistes lay among those mountains of paper. On the wooden walls hung photographs and framed letters of thanks from the authors whose work she had succeeded in placing. Elizabeth made a mental note that she must remember to send one herself.

'The Regina fans wouldn't like it or understand it,' Elizabeth suggested cautiously. 'Be honest, those novels have tended to be a trifle bland. Slightly predictable. Nobody could describe *Ramadan Mislaid* with those words. I know it's harder for you to place a first novel ...'

'That's not it at all. The first house I show this to will grab it. But you still owe Hodder a couple of novels under the current agreement and they've been very good to us.'

'Then offer it to them. Do a new deal for

Leslie Prince. Then, when the truth comes out as it inevitably will, they'll find they've got both authors. Come off it, Lisa, these things are going on all the time. Look at Anne Rice. Even Stephen King has played around with pseudonyms. I'm not trying to rip anybody off. It's just that there's so much extra baggage when my name is on the cover. This is the perfect way to destroy those preconceptions and let the book stand or fall in its own right. If nobody likes it, I can happily continue to churn out Regina novels until I drop. But if it gets the praise and attention I think it deserves, I can start writing better books with greater depth and miles more satisfaction.'

'So, it's really the critical appreciation you're after?'

'Absolutely. You and I both know this won't sell nearly as many copies as the rest of my stuff. But I think it's in a different league artistically and I want to find out whether I'm right.'

'It's a dangerous game, relying on the opinions of the critics. They are wrong just as often as they are right. And you know as well as I do that the crusade isn't getting the damn thing printed. Virtually nobody reviews a first novel. If I could bank a pound for every work I've truly believed in that's sunk without trace simply because nobody ever knew about it ...'

'Yes — and we've all done very nicely thanks to the works of Elizabeth Regina. But it's time to experiment. Look on this as a bonus.

Hodder aren't expecting another novel for months anyway. Just don't tell anyone that it's me. And there's no reason why, if it's a hit, I can't begin to make the Regina books more intriguing, more complex and more rewarding.'

'Well, if nothing else it should be fun. And I have to repeat, it's one hell of a fine novel. Disturbing, hilarious, significant ... and impossible to put down. You know what?' She lowered her voice. 'I think it could make the Booker shortlist.'

'You're joking! That would be the ultimate triumph.'

The Booker Prize was the biggest award a novelist could win. It came with prestige and publicity and hugely increased sales. It was shown on national television. It was commented on in the tabloid newspapers. Hitherto unknown writers became household names after appearing on the Booker shortlist. Acres of print; yards of privilege; very small financial remuneration in cash but immense increase in resultant earnings. The chances were pretty remote. Out of the hundreds of monthly releases, only half-a-dozen were selected to grace the shortlist and those picked very much relied on the idiosyncratic tastes of the judges.

'You realise what that would do... if a first novel won the Booker and then was revealed as being by a famous but unacclaimed popular writer under a pseudonym? You'd get the best of all possible worlds. But it's imperative that nobody, absolutely nobody, knows about this. Keep well away from all those gossips you consider friends.'

Elizabeth was momentarily disappointed that she wouldn't be able to see Kenneth Jenkins' face when he read *Ramadan Mislaid* but it was more than made up for by the thought of her triumph if it were to be shortlisted, let alone win. Either way, she had nothing to lose. She could always let him know the truth if the novel were to fail the selection process. She heaved a sigh of relief that she'd resisted her instinct to call and tell him what his passing comment had inspired. Actually, she'd already composed a cunning plot in her head involving a mutual but distant acquaintance who, she reckoned, could be relied upon to alert Kenneth to a new and interesting work of fiction. Jenkins adored being an early champion of young talent, especially if he was constantly given the credit for his astuteness.

'Go for it, girl!'

She could see that Lisa the Teaser's imagination had been completely captured. Her eyes were gleaming and she couldn't wipe the smile from her face, grinning like the Cheshire Cat.

'Oh yes; this could run and run. All the ingredients are there. It's politically correct. It covers other cultures — always popular with the critics. It's intelligent and beautifully crafted. It contains religion and sexuality and misery and unfairness. But, best of all, I really believe it deserves to win. I think it's one of the greatest works I've read all year — and in this job you read a lot!'

She swept her hand around the mounds of manuscripts in front of her. She gestured at the shelves groaning with fiction in every corner of her office.

Lisa Littlejohn raised her bone china blue-and-white Wedgwood tea cup and toasted Leslie Prince — 'our newest and finest novelist!'

Nine

The Surrey countryside was the absolute opposite of the sand dunes of the Sahara or the *souks* of Tangier.

Willings had been built in 1482. Originally three workmen's cottages, they had been knocked together during the Tudor era and converted with a giant central chimney providing heating for every room. The blazing fireplace opened on to each chamber and one wall in each bedroom baked hot as the bricks warmed.

The wooden beams and timbers had been slotted into each other so many centuries ago that they still bore the Roman numerals which had told the workmen which went where (and, interestingly, they had carved nine as VIIII rather than IX). The delightful odour of slightly charring wood and roasting stone permeated the house.

The large paddock and forest behind the house was home to rabbits, birds, voles and deer. It was quite common for Elizabeth to see white pheasants fluttering from the long grass into the branches of the trees.

The spaniels, delighted to be home after a fortnight of being pampered by the kennel owners, rushed maniacally around, sniffing and wagging and yelping and licking.

But there was something totally different now about Willings and Elizabeth knew exactly what it was. She had been changed so dramatically that her familiar surroundings were foreign to her.

Her nightly phonecalls to Kirk in Maria's Bar were becoming so lengthy that she could have purchased several round-trip tickets a week. She was certain of his motives and trusted him implicitly, but still she hesitated before taking the plunge.

The weeks became months. The days grew darker and longer. The festive season came and passed with dozens of gifts wrapped and couriered across the globe — both ways, to Elizabeth's delight — every one of her new-found friends sent her an inexpensive but genuinely thoughtful present.

She'd wanted to fly over for the holidays but the frantic pressures of proof-reading, editing, checking and changing, meeting and marketing, wheeling and dealing consumed her time. And there was the hesitant nervousness of not wanting to fall into it ... not wishing to risk killing the butterfly through indulgence ... 'Control yourself,' she told herself ... 'Give it time,' her friends advised ... and yet ... and yet ...

After one particularly amusing conversation, impressed as ever by Kirk's reticence to persuade her to do him any favours, she decided to see whether she could get him a visa to come to Britain.

Now began a series of visits to Ministries and embassies which involved numerous public relations executives, several Cabinet contacts, a couple of national newspaper editors and the host of a major radio talk show. Big buildings in Kensington, monolithic blocks in Whitehall, studios in Oxford Street, the BBC TV television centre ...

Red tape. Two small words but they bind the globe. Elizabeth became aware that 99.9% of the world exists only to avoid being noticed because then they might lose their jobs. So their daily grind is spent contorting and convoluting excuses, explanations, forms, reasons, problems and obstacles all blamed on somebody else.

She rapidly became used to the emotional experience. Positive delight on the phone. Bad tea at the meeting. Great enthusiasm for the project. Just a couple of minor potential difficulties. And they grew and grew. If she could bottle whatever it was that caused the difficulties to grow, she could revive the planet.

However, Elizabeth was not to be stopped. She fashioned the red tape into welcoming ribbons. The net result was the granting of an extended holiday visa for Kirk Kurabbi to visit the United Kingdom as the guest of Ms Elizabeth Regina.

She phoned that evening with the news. Considering it had been his life-long ambition, Kirk took it very calmly — grateful but not effusive. They discussed dates and flights and she was amused when he wondered which hotel he'd be staying in.

Ramadan Mislaid had been instantly accepted, as predicted, by Hodder Headline, and was being rushed into print. The usual, long, slow process had been expedited since Lisa the Teaser had already proclaimed her suspicion that this was a potential Booker short-lister. The allocated editor wanted no changes whatsoever. Readers had already begun spreading the word — Secker & Warburg, Little, Brown, Viking and Jonathan Cape had all called begging for the rights before they were signed.

The most extraordinary marketing and promotional campaigns, each virtually identical yet claiming originality, had been submitted. And rejected. The hard disk had been converted into all the necessary layout formats. The dust jacket and PR handout had been designed and Lisa had commented to Elizabeth that it was more like the release of a hit record than the normal publishing schedule.

'They are all desperate for a biography on Leslie Prince,' she said.

'So ... let's make one up, then,' answered Elizabeth, and together they composed a complete character.

Leslie Prince was born and raised in a working-class home. His parents saved pennies to educate him. Dad sweated down the mines. Mum scrubbed floors ('We must bring SCRUBBED FLOORS into it somewhere — they always do!'/'Couldn't we mention polishing doorsteps too?'/'No, that's too obvious.') An only child, he lost his parents just as he was due to go to Oxford on a well-deserved scholarship. Dad died of lung cancer ('The coal dust, you know,'); Mum died from a broken heart some months later ('Couldn't it be from overwork scrubbing all those floors?'/'Shut up, Elizabeth.')

After years of obscurity teaching literature in a terrible inner-city school pupilled mainly by illiterate blacks and Asians ('Isn't that racist?'/'Oh yes!') he scratched together this masterwork in his grubby attic ('Too blatant, scrap the attic,') and it's been turned down by every publisher in town until ...

That'll do.

By coincidence, Kirk was due to arrive at Heathrow on a GB Air flight on the day that the novel was scheduled for release.

Elizabeth prepared the nicest guest room at Willings for him because she wanted him to feel that he had his own privacy and space. The room, under the roof tiles, had its own en suite bathroom and toilet and was virtually self-contained. She found herself wondering whether she should have provided easy access facilities and then decided that such a consideration was the last thing Kirk needed.

She was well aware of the problems that Kirk's presence would create. Some of her friends and neighbours had been warned that a friend was coming to stay but she realised that his appearance would start every tongue in the county wagging. She doubted that any connection would be made between her young visitor and the protagonist of the new book by unknown novelist Leslie Prince, but was prepared to take precautions anyway. Kirk would be seen out as little as possible and would have to enjoy the pleasures of being closeted away in her exclusive company.

He understood this absolutely. She'd planned various outings, including, of course, a trip to Yorkshire, but since she was not that recognisable to the great British public, she had no fears of exposure.

Her closest confidante, Isobella, irritated anyway at having missed out on a Lanzarote holiday in the sun, but even more infuriated when Elizabeth had communicated certain intimate details of her Tangerine romance, was in a frenzy of curiosity. She'd been prepared for Kirk's physical deformities and shape, but was still nervously wondering what strange relationship had so affected her friend's character and lifestyle. Any description could merely hint at the reality.

They sat together eating traditional English muffins and crumpets and sipping cups of Earl Grey tea (tasting much nicer with the acceptable British milk and honey) in front of the blazing log fire, for autumn had turned to chill winter, as it tended to do within weeks at this time of year. Isobella tried to prise further information about Kirk out of Elizabeth, but only received raised eyebrows and innuendoes.

'You must simply wait until you meet him. He's a crippled half-caste with enormous energy and wit. He's funny and sensitive and intelligent, but he's also quite revolting-looking until you get to know him. Everybody will think he's after my money but I'm genuinely convinced he's not. Still, make up your own mind when you've spent some time with him. And, please, let me ask you again. Be discreet. Don't go gossiping.'

'As if I would! Don't you trust me? I'm your oldest friend!'

But even Isobella was not a party to the Leslie Prince scenario. That was intended to remain a secret between Lisa the Teaser, Elizabeth Regina and her friend, the crippled Arab.

Until they decided to announce the truth.

Ten

*T*he arrivals area at Heathrow Airport's Terminal One was not prepared for Kirk's presence.

Elizabeth had warned him on the phone to enter with a minimum of baggage — just the bare essentials, so as not to provoke Customs attention — and he was coming in on a simple two-week tourist visa. She stressed that it was vital he obeyed all the rules so that he would be automatically granted another visa and, eventually, more permanent access.

But nobody could stop Kirk Kurabbi from being himself.

He emerged from the Immigration and Customs sections into the greetings zone and saw Elizabeth waving from 100 yards away. Beaming with delight, he gesticulated at her, lost his hold on a crutch and crumpled helplessly to the ground, flapping about like a landed fish.

Observers fluctuated between wanting to rush to his aid and embarrassment at this ridiculous vision. Those offering him hands and support were rudely rejected as he thrashed around, attempting to regain his own stability. Sticks flailed in the air, catching policemen and taxi drivers on the shins and bringing down several would-be helpers.

Kirk was swearing and cursing in Arabic, a language particularly suited to obscenities being packed, as it is, with gutteral consonants.

This spectacular arrival eclipsed his otherwise discreet appearance. Elizabeth, of course, found the entire fiasco hilarious and roared with laughter, causing a similar reaction in Kirk, which was mistaken for hysteria by several medical assistants.

When, finally, she squeezed him into her car, they collapsed into the seats and gazed at each other in exhaustion.

'You certainly know how to make an entry!'

'I'm sorry, but that floor was like ice and I was so pleased to see you! Thank you for all this ... I really appreciate it.'

'I suppose you resent not being able to get around like everybody else.'

'Not at all — it might be different if this had happened when I was several years old but since I was born this way, it's normal for me. I feel sorry for you poor saps having to cope with those stiff legs propped up underneath you.

How on earth do you all manage?'

He chuckled in that individual way of his.

'You're certainly a one-off, Kirk. They broke the mould when they made you.'

'Wrong. They broke it *before* they made me!'

He was entranced by Willings. Somehow, the crooked, topsy-turvy little house reminded him of his own shape. He stroked the rough stonework and timbers. He was intrigued by the chimney and insisted on scrambling high up inside it to see the Priest's Hole, a tiny chamber which had secreted clerics from the search of the Cromwellian soldiers during the civil wars of the 17th century. Strangely, in that restricted and uncomfortable space, he was nimble and agile, using his arms and body, reminding her that the adults of the era had been smaller.

The spaniels adored him, licking and panting with delight at an obvious dog lover.

Elizabeth had organised a dinner party for his second night and her very closest friends, including Isobella, came to meet her strange new *protégé*.

Lewis McKenzie was a dour stockbroker who lived further along the leafy country lane which meandered over Leith Hill and down into the market town of Dorking. He and his wife Bridget were typical Surrey Conservatives, well dressed and manicured, three teenage children at public school, mainstays of the local community. A skeletal, mournful, cadaverous man, his spouse was vibrant, red-haired and vivacious.

Belinda Bellinger was a highly respected editor for Knopf on assignment in Great Britain. American, sassy and funny, she was a single girl in her late 40s who had made a career move from New York to London a decade ago and lived in an elegant Knightsbridge apartment just around the corner from The Lanesborough Hotel. Fashionably skinny, square-faced with a strong jawline and horsey bone structure, she wore designer frocks and the very latest stylish trainers in green, black and white.

Isobella de Valencia had married and divorced several times, acquiring a fortune and a beautiful mansion in the process. A silly woman, her heart was in the right place and, almost totally devoid of sense or seriousness, she provided Elizabeth with warmth and genuine companionship. She was enormously admiring of her friend's literary success and could have personified the type of readers that were described as devoted Regina fans. Overweight and over-made-up, she nonetheless brimmed with good humour.

The four of them arrived separately, desperate to check out this odd character. Kirk had been well briefed and was on best behaviour. He had allowed Elizabeth to find him a suitable maroon velvet smoking jacket with white shirt and bow tie and, hair combed neatly, looked very nearly acceptable for English country society. Seated next to the blazing log fire in the chintz drawing room, his crutches propped either side of the armchair, he was a disappointment to the inquisitive examiners of the exhibit.

They had expected a crazy wild man, out of control and unacceptable. Instead they found an urbane, witty, well-behaved young man, prepared to chatter and joke in the most sensitive way.

The meal went very well. Excellent food, fine wines, good company and gentle humour.

Lewis pontificated at length about the difference between the five North African territories. Morocco, a benign but autocratic monarchy, slowly improving the lot of the middle-class but still with serious problems of poverty and the social contrast between the extremely privileged Royal Family and the penniless peasants. Kirk remained discreet but informative, resisting any controversy.

'How about Algeria? The fundamentalist Islamics causing terrorism and murder. Then there's Libya with Gaddafi's rule alienating the West and provoking constant problems with the oil community. Egypt veers between the militants killing tourists and Mubarak trying to encourage his own view of democracy. And Tunisia, possibly the most stable society of all, yet sandwiched between the two military régimes in Algeria and Libya.'

Belinda added comments about the American attitudes and quoted extensively from Paul Theroux's latest travel book on the area. She found Kirk most intriguing and his observations revelatory.

At one point, confused by the political and social discussion, Isobella tried to bring the music and arts of the Mediterranean coast into the discussion, but, after a few polite remarks, the analysis of religion and business continued.

It was a successful evening. Lewis and Bridget were most impressed by Kirk's grasp of the ramifications, Belinda clearly found him attractive and Isobella decided she had some very astute acquaintances.

'I meant to tell you, darling,' she said to Elizabeth, 'I met another famous writer last night and he knows you, too. He's most charming. He's called Hathaway.'

Kirk and Elizabeth looked at each other.

'What time in the evening did you meet him?' asked Kirk.

'Right at the start,' answered Isobella, her chubby features beaming with delight at her remembered encounter. 'It was a dinner party for Gene and John Randall but I could only drop by for the drinks — I had a date to go to the theatre. Oh, he was most charming, most charming indeed. He spoke so highly of both of you. I've invited him to dine tomorrow night. You must all come. He's very well respected by those who know, I believe.'

Belinda had a previous appointment but the McKenzies accepted with pleasure. Kirk and Elizabeth felt they could hardly refuse but raised their eyes to the skies.

After the guests had left, Elizabeth gave Kirk an appreciative kiss.

'Thank you for behaving so well.'

'That's fine,' he said. 'They were all clearly anticipating the worst and I was determined to surprise them all by not being the outrageous character they expected. Sometimes it can be as rewarding confounding peoples' preconceptions as shocking them by behaving antisocially.'

She laughed. 'Don't let it affect you,' she grinned.

'Don't worry. I'm too old to change now,' he replied.

Eleven

*I*n addition to her flat in Eaton Square, Isobella had a huge mansion close to Willings and the guests gathered there for dinner the next night.

Lewis had already decided that he liked Kirk a lot. His wife was less sure and needed to be convinced but she was devoted to her husband, protective and loyal.

'Elizabeth — what a delightful coincidence! And Kirk — what a surprise! And a pleasure. So strange ... here ... in England.'

Henry R Hathaway was oozing charm from every pore though his pores were, as ever, not in the best of shape. He slimed his way around the guests, totally fooling Isobella who thought he was enchanting, though she wondered why his breath smelt so strongly of mint. He made certain to capture Lewis and his wife Bridget's attention by regaling them with tales of stocks and shares. He chortled at their jokes and flattered Isobella alarmingly. Wisely, he drank a minimum of alcohol, so the unpleasant aspect of his character failed to surface. He revealed to Isobella's delight that his latest novel included certain ideas inspired by Ms Regina herself, stolen 'with permission, of course' whilst they had spent time together in Tangier. Elizabeth and Kirk grinned in their shared private knowledge.

It appeared that Venom's book was to be published in a couple of months, some while after Leslie Prince's.

The de Valencia pile was set on the hill overlooking Willings — it could be clearly seen from Elizabeth's garden, white columns, proud façade, flights of steps, manicured lawns. Inside, it was rather cold though luxuriously appointed. Antiques and *objets d'art* abounded. Isobella made sure to show everyone to her new friend.

After dinner, the McKenzies invited everybody back to their home where they took coffee and were regaled by pictures of absent teenagers and mutual acquaintances. Lewis and Kirk became deeply and animatedly engaged in conversation. HRH, as he liked to be called, wandered around the house on his own whilst Elizabeth, Isobella and Bridget indulged in girl talk. When it came to squealing with laughter, Bridget McKenzie could cackle for Canada. It was an amusing game making her laugh. Kirk and Lewis smiled at the eruptions of merriment interrupting their financial discussions. Venom had gone missing but he returned soon enough. As they all parted, Elizabeth grinned at Kirk and said, 'Well, Venom behaved himself for once and can you believe we both managed not to reveal his nickname?'

Kirk was as passionate in England as he'd been in Tangier but their relationship had become much more personal. They spoke at length to each other, again and again. The fondness had increased; the lust had levelled out. He also explained that his homosexual inclinations appeared to have slackened off.

'Quite often I only used to do it for financial reasons,' he explained, 'and now that seems a poor excuse. I've seen a few guys I've found physically attractive, but the effort didn't seem justified by the reward anymore. What I've found with you is an affection, a warmth, a comfort and a pleasure. Suddenly, on its own, physical satisfaction appears superficial and a bit empty.'

As a result, he'd concentrated in Morocco in cleaning up his rooms, doing chores for Maria, earning a few dirhams working at Jock's place and considering plans for his future. That future definitely included Elizabeth, but only if she wanted it to.

'Every other Moroccan boy dreams of finding a wealthy widow, or the equivalent, ready to be seduced in return for rewarding him with cash, presents and a life in a society which will grant him the potential to better himself. But that's never interested me. I never watched the queens and thought of tricking them into a phony relationship. Somehow, to me, that's as bad as rape. Even worse. You're being dishonest with a person's dreams and that's very, very bad karma. Let them enjoy you and pay you but don't lie to them emotionally.'

It was his honesty she loved most.

The one outing he was truly anticipating with joy was upon them. Into the car, packed lunch ready in the hamper from Fortnum and Mason, boiled brown eggs, York ham, chicken sandwiches, Perrier for her and White Riesling for him, pewter tankards frothing with ice chilled in a cooler, cakes and hot tea in a separate thermos, linen and china and silverware. Up the motorway to the north, pausing half-way to consume their repast in a field. Back on to the M1. Past Leeds. Off the M1 towards Wetherby.

Kirk was bouncing up and down in his seat as the misty green meadows rolled past. He loved the grey slate walls and stone fences. He wound down his window to breathe in the damp, cool air as though it was pure oxygen. It was so alien to the dusty, sandy atmosphere of North Africa, yet his soul could feel the kindred spirit as clearly as Heathcliff's search for the ghost of Cathy. Even the sheep looked different from their Moroccan counterparts. Here they were fluffy lambs. Over there they resembled pot-smoking hippies, wise and elderly, informing the shepherds exactly what they should be doing.

They booked into the Wood Hall Hotel in Linton, a huge Georgian mansion with 43 rooms and special facilities for the disabled, a luxury he'd never experienced before. They drove towards Sicklinghall and parked just off the A661 at the edge of a wood dangling above a small valley. That was where Kirk's mother had been born and raised. That's where she grew and was schooled, learned her languages and attitudes, had her first boyfriends and made her first mistakes. They could see the little farm nestling beneath them, smoke dutifully curling from a smokestack. Kirk didn't want to visit his relations. He had no desire to communicate with those who had totally disowned him and had helped bruise his mother's heart. He had no interest at all in cousins or grandparents or uncles or aunts. They would only shy away from him in horror anyway. He merely wanted to experience the atmosphere of the area. He'd enjoyed hearing the soft, northern vowels of people working in the motorway petrol stations. He'd demanded typical scones and flat pancakes for tea. He smelt the earth on his fingers and lay flat in the green grass examining the leaves and plants. He tuned in to the local radio station just so he could hear the regional advertisements.

He'd spent hours in tiny local village shops, filtering through packages and products. And he sat silent in the car for several hours, thinking his own thoughts whilst Elizabeth strolled around the nearby trees, leaving him to deal with his past and his present.

He was subdued that night, but they had a first-class meal of roast leg of lamb (English) and Barbary duck (Barbarian) with crisp skin and succulent pink meat, followed by crêpes filled with warm berry compôte and almond cream.

In their room, they talked. They talked about his longings and his frustrations and his emptiness at not having a family and a background. And all of a sudden, he noticed that Elizabeth was quietly crying.

'What's the matter? Don't worry. I'll be fine.'

But the silent tears turned to choking sobs. Kirk held her in his arms and stroked her back to calm her.

'It was tears for myself. I realised how lucky I've been to find you. You're so genuine, so honest. And then it came back to me why I've never allowed myself to feel any depth of emotion. My parents rarely gave me any true affection, yet I was shattered when they were killed out of the blue. Oh, I put on a brave face — to myself as well as to the outside world. I pretended I didn't mind; I'd never been close to them anyway. But deep down inside, subconsciously, I was wrecked. I'd never again have the chance to love, to feel passion, to care. They had been dragged out of my life in the most brutal fashion — a car crash. And we'd never communicated. I justified my sensible response and convinced myself I just never felt anything below the surface. But you've brought out those depths in me. You've made me realise, at this late stage of life, that I can feel and love and hurt and care as well as anyone else. Your quest for your roots has helped me find my own genuine nature.'

He stroked her gently.

'So, after all the blatant differences have been removed, we're quite the same, really.'

They slept dreamlessly in a suite filled with fresh flowers and returned quietly the next day to Surrey.

Elizabeth had the strong feeling that several demons had been laid to rest.

Twelve

*L*isa the Teaser was losing control.

'I've never had such a response to a novel, first or otherwise,' she complained, 'and I can't provide anybody with interviews or information. That *Booked* programme on Channel Four is desperate to devote an entire show to Leslie Prince — understandably, since their target audience consists almost entirely of gays, minorities and paraplegics — and I've had to fob them off with lame excuses. Hodder are going spare. It's done 25,000 in hardback in a week — that's ten times the expected amount. Fortunately, somebody had the foresight to print more copies on release. This is the publishing hit of the year. And I can already anticipate problems.

'The buzz is that it's going to be nominated as the Whitbread winner of the Best First Novel category. Well, of course, we can't allow that to happen. We'll be done for fraud!'

They chuckled.

'Meantime, I'm faxing you a dozen sheets of questions that need answers — they are the next best thing to interviews and will tax your inventive powers to the limit. You've got to work out Leslie's favourite holiday destinations, his taste in women, preferred colour of underpants, food allergies, weather dislikes, film top ten and hundreds of other useless enquiries. I tell you what — when you've finished creating Leslie Prince, there'll be another novel waiting to be written!'

'How's it looking on the Booker front?' asked Elizabeth.

'You never can tell, because it's down to the vagaries of the judges, but I'd bank on it getting nominated. The good thing is that, since we rush-released it, it's due for consideration this year and the Booker ceremony is before the others ... if we gear everything towards that, we can reveal Leslie's true identity and let everyone cope after the announcement.'

'The reviews have been fantastic. If nothing else, I've proved myself on that front. Did you believe *The Sunday Times* this weekend?'

The Sunday Times have a weekly Book Review section specialising in populist but critically admired works normally penned by famous writers and reviewed by a cluster of minor celebrities. They had raved about *Ramadan*

Mislaid, giving it their Front Page slot and allocating the review to Jefferson Dubris, the acclaimed serious historian specialising in Islamic works for the London School of Economics. He had praised the novel to the skies — for its accuracy, its technical power, its characterisation, its humanity and its entertainment value. The accompanying illustration of a handsome, romantic, darker Kirk had caused great amusement over the eggs and coffee that morning.

'Yes. And how about *The Literary Review* and *The Spectator*?' added Lisa.

Even the tabloids — the *Daily Mail* and *Express* — had picked up on *Ramadan Mislaid* and recommended it to their readers. It contained all the qualities and ingredients currently intriguing the public.

'Now can you make sure you fill in those questionnaires and fax them back to me tomorrow?'

'In a day or two perhaps ...'

'No, Mr Prince — tomorrow. It's bad enough having to do all this without a real person around to milk the publicity. The least you can do is provide me with prompt and enticing replies!'

Meanwhile, Elizabeth and Kirk shared their final few days of the visit together. They had discovered more and more chunks of common ground and fewer areas of disagreement. Kirk had come to know Willings very well. He sat for hours taking in the ancient vibrations from the walls. He was positive that the ghosts and spirits of 500 years remained comfortable in the building. He constantly chose to walk the spaniels around the paddock and they were wildly attached to him. But he was also perfectly prepared to return to Tangier and had spoken several times on the phone to the team in Morocco. His current situation had revealed a placid level deep in his soul. After removing the angst of his disturbed Yorkshire roots, he'd become much more at peace with himself.

And their bedroom sessions were getting longer and fonder, with less physical activity and more stroking, tickling, caressing and cuddling.

She was enthralled by his body. At rest, supine, it was perfectly proportioned and very muscular though, as you looked closely, many of the strengths and tendons were in the wrong places. The body hair was the shading of a master, da Vinci at his most sensitive. And his face, though hideous by definition, had a beauty in its ugliness. He could have posed as one of Pan's cherubs, the goat-hoofed creature of the pipes, debauched yet innocent, devilish but angelic. A youth of contrasts, endlessly absorbing.

'What on earth am I doing here?' he asked her one evening, as they sprawled on the rug in front of the roaring fire. It was a chilly spring evening and they had stacked the logs high. The cracking flames warmed the entire house. The spaniels were in seventh heaven. They adored the smell and the heat and the cosiness.

'What do you mean?'

'Well, I'm an Arab half-breed who belongs in Morocco. I was born and brought up there. I look Arabic. I speak and think in Arabic. I'm totally out of place here. You're making a fool of yourself with a toy-boy who is half your age and as ugly as sin. None of it makes any sense.'

Then they caught each other's eye and burst into laughter. Of course it made no sense. It was mad. Insane. Crazy. But it was reality and there was nothing they could, or wanted to, do about it.

Very kindly, Henry R Hathaway had sent a pre-release signed copy of the manuscript of his new novel *Lavender Condoms* over to them. They had read it together. It was quite dreadful. Pretentious, inflated, significant and arch. Kirk had commented that, in many ways, he'd have written it better if he'd been drunk.

'At least when he's being poisonous he's occasionally entertaining.'

'They will probably make a highly successful, unseen art movie out of it again,' said Elizabeth. 'It does owe an awful lot to a little-known Hemingway short story, but who will ever point that out?'

When the time came for his return to Tangier, she drove him to the airport and watched as he cleared the boarding controls.

'Soon you'll be back,' she'd said, 'but before that I want to come over to visit you and Eddie and Maria and the gang again. So tell them to prepare for another invasion!'

He waved goodbye — more carefully than before and they both grinned at the memory — and shuffled sadly out of sight.

Thirteen

The judging panel for The Booker Prize consisted of various critics from the *Observer*, the *Telegraph*, the *Independent* and *The Sunday Times*, alongside a couple of MPs and a TV journalist.

They met for lunch at the Chairman's house and began slotting the various contenders into piles for perusal.

Hundreds of books were entered for consideration and it was a Herculean task to read every word of every one but the judges set to with a vengeance, consuming several a day and eliminating dozens an hour. Bad writing, copied themes, unlikely names, non-politically-correct attitudes, sloppy similes — reasons for rejection were frequently the same as those for selection, depending on the attitude of the expert involved.

Worthy and dedicated, they were ploughing

their way through the hundreds of contenders.

Odd, individual choices were praised and abandoned. One of the judges, a lady with strong liberal sympathies, went overboard for a bizarre novel featuring every possible kind of drug hallucination and praising experimentation with chemical substances as the finest purpose for life. Unfortunately, it was written so badly as to be incomprehensible to the other esteemed critics, who insisted on dropping it despite her heartfelt pleas and genuine tears. At one point, she had to be comforted, so affected was she by the rejection of her favourite.

There were those who could not consume Salman Rushdie under any circumstances (an unusual but, surprisingly, large category amongst the general public) whereas most of the critics felt he was Britain's greatest living writer. Just. There were fans of the surreal and admirers of the obtuse. Those who loved good plots and those who felt deep subtexts and intricate characterisation should be the key ingredients.

From a vast field of hundreds, they had whittled the list down to a mere 30 or 40. *Ramadan Mislaid* remained in there, poised to make the eventual shortlist of half-a-dozen fortunate titles.

The ultimate selection was to take place over a meal at the Chairman's home.

Hartley Partigan MP (for Bournemouth) was a Conservative whose part time position as leader of a children's charity and esteemed work as a local magistrate combined with his connections to various publishing organisations to make him the perfect choice as non-voting Chairman and host of the event. He was, it must be said, an expert in the art of compromise, a talent vital both to his current situation and to his career as a politician.

His house was a formal Edwardian terrace building in Westminster. Mr Partigan, a handsome man with gleaming, even white teeth and a ready smile to reveal them, sat at the head of the table, golden locks dangling attractively over his unlined brow. Roast beef and trimmings were served by butlers and waiters. The judges had gathered in the dining-room and sipped their drinks while proposing their three individual choices. This was the ultimate slimming-down process. Eventually, the handful of trimmed titles would suffer the final cut and six would be abandoned.

As luck would have it, three novels had been chosen by several of the judges — multiple choices were virtually bound to go through — and *Ramadan Mislaid* was one of them.

The *Telegraph* critic, a crusty, irritable, humourless man called Tony Jones, hated it and argued that it conformed to far too many of the conventions, had clearly been written simply to contain every element of past winners ('Look at the sex scenes — pure Pat Barker ...') and did not really deserve inclusion. The others praised it, however, and it was clearly a majority choice for the shortlist. Indeed, when the final six were eventually chosen, after much more discussion, large quantities of alcohol consumed and the near spilling of blood mingling with the port and cheese, Leslie Prince ('Who is he anyway? There's a rumour it's a pseudonym. I hope this isn't going to embarrass us ...') was solidly there.

Lisa got the news early and called Elizabeth in terrific excitement.

'We've done it! It really doesn't matter now whether we win it or not. The sales will go through the roof — it's already far and away the biggest seller of the six and this critical credibility will boost the popular attention. I think you can rest assured that you've achieved your ambition, Elizabeth. You have proved you're a great writer as well as a commercial one.'

They agreed that total silence would be retained and that A P Watt would invite Elizabeth, as one of their writers, to the ceremony at the Guildhall, just in case Leslie Prince won, in which case she would reveal all by accepting the award and astonishing the gathered literary world. Requests for photos and further biographical detail were avoided, driving the organisers crazy.

'Leslie is a very private man,' Lisa explained. 'He believes his work speaks for itself and doesn't want any of the celebrity attached to fame. He will, however, attend the prize-giving and will be available to collect his award, if he wins.'

This was simply not good enough for the Booker people and even less acceptable to the BBC, who liked being able to do filmed profiles and set up camera angles for their live TV coverage. But Lisa explained there was simply no alternative.

'He is shy. He keeps a low profile. He says everything you need to know about him is written in the chapters of his work. Simply quote the novel if you want to talk about him. No photos. No interviews. And a simple statement that he's flattered and delighted by the selection of his *Ramadan Mislaid* for the final Booker shortlist.'

Of course, the mystery and intrigue increased as a result of his unavailability. As with Elvis Presley, the less easy the subject is to reach, the more the media desires them. And Lisa had to field the most extraordinary requests, calls and even having her Rolladex rifled by hacks searching for a contact number or clue as to Mr Prince's whereabouts.

WHO IS LESLIE PRINCE? howled the headlines. Even the tabloids joined the chorus, which, obviously, delighted the Booker organisers, more than making up for their irritation at his lack of availability.

Meanwhile, there was serious trouble brewing. Henry R Hathaway, whose latest novel had been critically castigated on publication, had been abandoned and deserted early in the process. Failing even to make the Booker shortlist, with sales lower than ever and his reputation seriously damaged, Venom had taken firmly to the bottle and the darker side of his complex character had regained the upper hand.

Spitting bile at every opportunity, he was working on a plot to damage and destroy as many people as he possibly could. And with his considerable abilities harnessed by demons, the resulting inferno could be expected to make a nuclear holocaust look like a damp firework.

Elizabeth had decided, after Kirk's totally successful visit to Britain, that she would return to Tangier sooner rather than later. The months of waiting had proved unnecessary. Her instincts were correct. This was her destiny. Determined and delighted, she grasped it with both hands.

Fourteen

*E*lizabeth organised her trip to Morocco like The Lady Bountiful.

In a frenzy of buying, she rushed from store to store across London, gathering gifts for her new friends. Her hotel was booked, she was scheduled on a flight, the spaniels were once more allocated to the kennels and Elizabeth prepared to return to her beloved North African coast.

She had hired a car through Avis's international booking agency. It cost a fortune but she very much wanted to see more of the country this time. She stuffed the red and white documents under the seat and remembered to keep to the right as she swerved past unco-operative camels and recalcitrant hens. The dark storm clouds she'd flown through evaporated as swiftly as they'd arrived and the sky was pure blue, clear and crisp. After greeting the team with mutual ecstasy, kissing Eddie on his gin-flavoured chops, wrapping her arms around Maria's generous proportions and delivering the bumper bundle of gifts, they sat down at the familiar table to consume the meal of Maria's best seafood.

There was a lot of gossip to catch up on.

'That dreadful Venom's been here again,' said Maria, 'snapping away with his horrid instamatic and poking his nose in left, right and centre.'

Jock coughed loudly. 'He's och man ya doon nibod cairn,' he articulated.

'Jock doesn't like him either,' explained Eddie. 'His new novel is called *Lavender Condoms*. Sounds prickly to me.'

Elizabeth told them about their chance encounter with HRH in England.

'It's never a chance encounter where Venom's concerned,' sneered Eddie. The man had been asking many too many questions about all their backgrounds for his liking.

'SPS,' said Maria, tapping her nose.

'SPS?' asked Elizabeth.

'Small Penis Syndrome,' answered Maria. 'I've seen it so many times. Sociologists and psychiatrists go on about "It's not what you've got, it's what you do with it." Bollocks! Men with tiny dicks have massive chips on their shoulders. And Venom's is smaller than most — I have my sources! Married three times and rapidly divorced — the moment his poor wives discovered the matchstick, I reckon!'

They roared with laughter.

Elizabeth and Kirk set off on a grand tour, destined to culminate in the legendary Hotel Mamounia in Marrakech.

Their first stop was at the beautiful city of Fès, originally a regional capital and spectacular, both inside the bordering pink stone walls and from the hills outside, looking down on the town. They stayed at the Palais J'nan, a new luxury residence with first-class facilities and gardens, pools and restaurants, done up in an old-fashioned style like a medieval palace. A day excursion took them to Meknès, a lesser-known but equally pretty town, and they sipped mint tea on the terrace of the Hotel Angleterre, watching the sunset beyond the ramparts of the city, nibbling at finger sandwiches and cherishing the beauty of the view.

The contrasts between the tourist areas and the real life of the Moroccans was extraordinary. Kirk, being well aware of the true Arab lifestyle, made sure that Elizabeth saw both sides of the culture. The shops and sights were colourful but predictable; the homes and narrow lanes considerably more atmospheric. She ate all the local nameless delicacies, drank soups that tasted like over-spiced thin goulash, painted her face and hands with henna, and wore the loose robes of the native Arab women. She found the experience enormously enriching.

Then down to Rabat, the capital, on the Atlantic ocean — a Geneva-styled enclave full of embassies and diplomats. Far and away the most international of the Moroccan cities, the Royal Palace dominated the area and there were more European-standard hotels and eateries. The boulevards were wider, cleaner and less crammed with peasant transport. Many black sedans zoomed past, carrying ambassadors and consuls, secretaries and press attachés in air-conditioned quiet.

The road to Casablanca was an excellent motorway and they reached the largest city in an hour. After the vast expanse of suburbs, factories, ports and beaches, they arrived at the centre, dominated by the giant mosque, towering over the casbah and clearly visible from every corner. Every road seemed to lead to the mosque. Whichever way they turned, there it was, looming high above everything.

They stayed at the Hyatt and ate in Wang Chung, enjoying the Chinese cuisine. They took aperitifs in the Casablanca Bar where Hoagy Carmichael tunes were played on the piano. Hanging on the walls were prints from the movie with Humphrey Bogart putting a friendly arm round Claude Rains' shoulders. They felt this was the start of a beautiful friendship.

On to Marrakech, the winding road getting dustier and drier as they came further into the central southern region of the country. Olive and orange groves lay planted, acre after acre. Some big, round fruit dangled pendulous from the branches. The ground turned redder, a kind of rich ochre colour, and the plains stretched flat for miles. The heat increased. It was now pleasantly warm, T-shirt weather, though the inhabitants still wore the thick woollen jellabas with hoods masking their faces and bright scarves wrapped around their necks. The Mamounia, Winston Churchill's favourite, had just undergone a face lift. It was elegant, stuffy and pretentious, though very comfortable and luxurious as well. Brocade, embroidery, satins and silks; velvet couches; crystal ashtrays; gold-finished glass goblets; deep blue sunbeds beside the pool. Since the dining-room required evening dress, they ate in their suite, listening to the BBC World Service.

They strolled down to the D'Jema El Fna, the famous square photographed more times than the Mona Lisa's smile and considerably more enigmatic, a colourful array of acrobats, snake charmers, pick-pockets, villains, salesmen, spice dealers, smells, tastes and patterns. Even in these places, where Kirk was not known at all, the locals respectfully kept away from them, reserving their pestering for the more obvious tourists.

After a few days, they continued their motorised tour, taking in Agadir, an ugly, modern collection of buildings erected after the town was totally destroyed in a 1960s earthquake, and finished with a week in nearby Taroudannt at the magnificent Gazelle d'Or Hotel, regarded by many as the best in the world.

The entire trip was relaxing, enjoyable and intimate. They flew back to Tangier, leaving the car at Agadir airport, and rejoined Eddie and Maria for several more days before Elizabeth took her leave and returned to London.

It had been one of the least stressful and most pleasurable holidays of her life. Accepted as a local character, she felt as much at her ease as she ever did in the peaceful downs of Surrey. They took a taxi to Tangier airport, and as she kissed Kirk goodbye, she raised an eyebrow and predicted that it was the quiet before the storm.

They could not have known just how right she was.

Part 3

Fifteen

*N*ow it was getting silly.

It had started as an intelligent discussion over each judge's personal selection as the Booker Prize winner. *Ramadan Mislaid* and the last part of a trilogy about farmers in a remote French wine-growing village had both been chosen by two of the critics. Tony Jones, however, had gone for the least popular of the half-dozen contenders, a morbid fantasy about a serial killer's devotion to his dog, which the others hated. It had only got this far through his championship. A willingness to accept opposing views over the months had allowed the judges to further it continually but now they were putting their feet down, coming out of their liberal closets and universally condemning it.

'If there's one novel I will never give the prize to, this is it,' declared Bella O'Shaughnessy, the *Observer* critic, with suitably appalling grammar. 'It's a repugnant book.'

'So why did you agree for it to grace the shortlist?' sneered Jones. He was a white man — a shock of white hair; white skin creased with white lines; his clean white hands and white shirt cuffs stuck out of an off-white, shabby Italian suit. Now in his 60s, he looked in his late 80s and terminally in need of colour.

'Because you loved it so much,' shouted Bella, in astonishment. 'We agreed that any novel provoking 100% enthusiasm deserved serious consideration and this crap won through because, when the crunch came, none of the titles outside the five chosen inspired such devotion from any of us. But compared to the other contenders, this piece of crap stinks.'

'Hear, hear,' muttered the *Independent* representative, nervously.

'Well, I'm not voting for anything else,' hissed Jones, 'they're rubbish.'

'It doesn't have to be a unanimous choice,' soothed Hartley Partigan MP, stroking his hair as though it was the *Telegraph* man's ego, 'but it seems clear that *Bodies and Bones* is not going to get a majority vote, so let's move on to *The Soldier's Story*. Now this has been admired by ...'

Andy Jefferson, the BBC reporter for *Arena*, *Panorama* and *The Book Programme*, mentally switched off and took to wondering whether Mr Partigan was aware of the fact that several investigative journalists knew about his liaison with Fenella Devine, a hooker specialising in bondage and whipping, who provided her services to various Members of Parliament from a flat across the river from the House of Commons. A senior executive of *The People*, whose personal tastes caused him never to make excuses or leave, had seen him arriving just after one of his own rather expensive sessions. It was more a question of 'when' than 'whether', pondered Andy. Mrs Partigan was not going to be pleased.

Hartley was pontificating at length, smiling and preening, pouring tea and presiding graciously.

Bella. An attractive woman. Well dressed, intelligent, a good writer. Married with three young children. Having a lesbian affair, Andy happened to know. Indeed, she'd been doing so for several years. Nothing wrong with that, if discreet.

Very little to know about Jones. That was the trouble. Perhaps a few skeletons in his closet might mean one less in that appalling suit.

He couldn't remember the name of the *Independent* person.

John Gale from *The Sunday Times* observed Jefferson watching his fellow judges. No real reason for him to be here, thought Gale. A pretend intellectual. Promoted at the Beeb because of his looks rather than his brains. A handsome guy. Hair nicely trimmed. Casual clothes, slightly younger in style than his mid-30s persona. Very thick eyebrows — not bushy but going straight across above his nose. Pretty features. Will get chubby later in life, and start to look as though he's melting. Mildly effeminate. Not surprising since, rumour had it, he frequented gay bars and enjoyed being picked up by truck drivers.

'So which is your choice, John?'

'It has to be *Ramadan Mislaid*, Hartley. A brilliant novel but it's also populist and entertaining. It has depth and intelligence. It's incredibly well written. Head and shoulders above the rest.'

'Oh, come on, Gale,' spat Tony Jones, 'we can't choose that one. It's full of tokenism. Every time Rushdie puts out a book, he's selected. This year, thank God, he's not published, so we give the award to another Islamic-based work. We'd be laughed out of business.'

'I don't agree at all,' chimed Isaac Anderson, the other MP on the panel and an acclaimed biographer. 'The fact that there are Arabs in it has nothing to do with Salman's novels. It's a human story, fascinating and funny. That's why I think we should go for it. It's been ages since wit cropped up in a Booker Prize winner. Remember that bloody awful First World War thing they picked a few years ago — all misery and symbolism and depressing description? Let's give it to this genuinely humorous triumph.'

'I don't know that it's a triumph,' said Bella. 'It's very much a man's book. There's no real understanding of the female psyche in it. Now the Wyatt novel, on the other hand ...' — this was the other multiple choice favourite — 'has incredible sensitivity. The way those women are described, picking the grapes and coping with the pressures of a small French village ...'

You'd probably be a good fuck, thought Hartley Partigan MP, watching her hand gestures. Dress you up in a headmistress's outfit, give you a cane and a pair of *pince-nez* ... Hmmm.

They discussed and argued and squabbled and sulked. Tables were pounded. Irreversible positions were struck and abandoned. Bella grew weepy at one point and said they should never have dismissed *The Hallucinogenic Helix*. Hartley thought she looked less attractive when she was being soft. Opinions veered back and forth but, when the final votes were counted, Leslie Prince came through as the clear winner.

'You'll all live to regret it,' grumbled Jones who, nonetheless, had clinched the decision by casting his ballot against the Wyatt novel — 'a dreary story all about menstruation.'

Sixteen

*L*isa the Teaser had organised a large table at the Guildhall for the agency and Elizabeth had requested two seats at it, one for herself and one for Kirk, whom she intended to bring over for the Booker ceremony.

'Are you sure that's wise?' asked Lisa. 'When people see him, they'll immediately put two and two together.'

'Not necessarily,' said Elizabeth, 'they'll probably think he's Leslie Prince himself. Don't forget, you've promised he'll be attending the event in case he wins. So they will all be trying to work out who he is.'

Kirk was already booked for his second flight, visas cleared and paperwork in order. The journey took place and Elizabeth collected him from Heathrow, this time without further problems.

He was clearly starting to consider himself at home at Willings, decorating his room with pictures and posters of his own taste, but Elizabeth still felt very comfortable about him. Despite his frightening honesty and occasional bursts of biliousness about fate, the British Government and inequality, he blended into her Surrey life incredibly well. And he constantly grilled her as to whether she felt pressurised or utilised.

'The moment you start having doubts about my motives, whether or not they are groundless, you tell me and I'm hopping straight back to Tangier. No right-minded person thinks there's any other reason for my friendship with you than greed and a desire to further myself by making you fall in love with me. If you even suspect that, say the word and I'm off. Because we can survive that suspicion but only if we nip it in the bud by killing it with honesty. You worry — I go, and we can try to pick up the pieces weeks, months or years later.'

Isobella and he got on very well. Her friend was flattered by his questions about her world and impressed by his sensitivity. He, in turn, never patronised or talked down to her, though he was clearly much brighter than her. Isobella's friendship with Henry R Hathaway had cooled distinctly.

One evening, during a dinner just after the publication and crucifixion of his novel, he had drunk far too much and his truly venomous nature had been revealed. He'd started by criticising her friends and then had rounded on her, moving the good-natured soul to tears. Ever since then, she had refused his calls. She was delighted to discover his nickname.

Lewis McKenzie liked Kirk very much indeed, finding his astute mind refreshing. He offered unusual opinions from a newly-informed viewpoint, managing to see the woods for the trees, and Lewis often called round to put a question to him and have it considered in a different way. They would sit together, the gloomy, dark, thin stockbroker and the ugly, rubber-faced, gesticulating half-caste, analysing and dissecting.

In return for Kirk's intelligent, if amateur, advice, Lewis had insisted in investing a thousand pounds on the stock exchange for him. Kirk had only agreed to this as long as Lewis promised to repay himself the thousand if it multiplied. He came over brimming with pleasure and delight to inform Kirk and Elizabeth that, 'totally due to Kirk's clever assessment of the details I gave him ...' his grand had grown a hundredfold. Literally within a month, Kirk had earned a hundred thousand pounds — or ninety nine, as he corrected.

Elizabeth and Kirk discussed most things. They felt enormously comfortable with each other. Sometimes Kirk would return to his outrageous, flamboyant persona and Elizabeth loved it. He made her laugh. One morning he'd dress in her clothes and put on heavy make-up. Another would see him suited and attired like a city gentleman.

The spaniels didn't mind what he looked like, what he wore or how he behaved. With their undemanding, gentle natures they had decided he was one of them, to be loved and appreciated without qualifications. They wagged their stumpy little golden tails, panted and slavered, barked and squeaked and politely asked whether he felt like taking them walkies.

That's what dogs are for.

Walkies was another different experience for Kirk, manfully struggling through the mud and clumps of damp long grass, but he refused any help.

Belinda Bellinger came to dinner one night, got slightly pissed and definitely tried to flirt with him. The more wine she consumed, the closer she sat until she could no longer resist touching him.

Elizabeth was both amused and intrigued to watch Kirk's reaction. He handled her deftly, kindly and without any offence. After she'd driven away, rather unsteadily, they said they hoped she'd be safe on the road and he commented that he'd found her attention flattering.

'I can never understand people getting upset when someone fancies them,' he said. 'The English are particularly good at being offended. When some queen approaches a boy, he reacts as though he's suffered the worst insult in the world whereas, in fact, it's a compliment. Could anything be more morale-boosting than another human being telling you they find you attractive? You can always decline the advances in a polite way. Very few people push it and, if they do, you can make your refusal clearer.'

'It's easier for a guy than a girl,' commented Elizabeth.

'Perhaps so, but the basic premise is still true. Appealing to somebody is a nice thing, not a nasty one.'

'Some people may see it as a threat.'

'Well, they shouldn't do. 99 times out of 100 it's simply a tribute.'

Belinda had said something rather disturbing during the evening. She knew of their experiences with Venom and had encountered his editor some days ago.

'He was telling me how ghastly Hathaway can be,' she'd said, 'and told me some story about how much he hated you and was planning to ruin your lives. Watch out for him. He's a nasty piece of work. Even his greatest fans admit he's a poisonous creep in person.'

Lisa Littlejohn came for lunch. She was nervous about meeting the legendary Kirk, though his name had, of course, been changed in Leslie Prince's novel, since she was not too sure how much was invention and how much truth in the literary creation.

Elizabeth knew when Lisa felt uncomfortable because she toyed with her spectacles and fingered the neck of her smart, matching suit. But, as in most other cases, Kirk won her over very quickly. As they drank coffee in front of the log fire, Lisa remarked that she was looking forward to his company at the Booker Prize Award dinner.

'I don't think too many people will put two and two together at the event,' she said. 'The character in the book is much more over the top. Yes, there are the obvious similarities but, for example, your protagonist in *Ramadan Mislaid* is fair-haired and blue-eyed, clearly in order to stress the English side of his birthright. There may be whispers but I don't think it matters. Anyway, the moment the winner is announced, one way or the other, win or lose, the game is up. I think we then want to declare that Leslie Prince is Elizabeth Regina. There will be terrific publicity which will help sell many more copies. And, after the secret is revealed, you can happily let the world know that Kirk and you are, as they say, an item.'

'Yes — that's been the only disadvantage of all this,' said Elizabeth. 'Most of our closest friends know but we've got nothing to be ashamed of and we'd both like to be able to legitimise our relationship.'

'Having now met your young man, I can't blame you, dear,' said Lisa the Teaser with a smile, and Kirk laughed with flattered pleasure.

Seventeen

The Guildhall was the most beautiful venue in London for prestigious events. Rich, dark-wood panelling and impressively carved, ornate pillars and furnishings, it had been there for centuries. Magnificently decorated tables crammed the floor, laid meticulously with crisp napkins and engraved silverware. Hundreds of representatives of the cream of intelligentsia and the creative arts murmured politely into each other's ears. Dinner jackets, black bow ties, starched shirts, polished shoes, evening dresses, subtle jewellery.

The BBC had set up cameras capable of capturing every angle. The expert commentators were grouped in a box overlooking the scene beneath through thick panes of sound-proofed glass, like intellectual goldfish gasping at the sea floor. They rattled through the six contenders, analysing the authors and describing the plots. The hostess was allowed red-rimmed spectacles in a daring concession to rebellion.

One curly, grey-haired bow tie muttered softly about grandeur, symbolism and passion without a shred of emotion. A tall, willowy but gnarled Australian lady clutched at her wrinkled neck and hated things. An Irish wit with sparkling eyes seduced the camera and smiled at viewers.

The classy, intelligent, artistic and refined aura of calm and measured critical assessment permeated the hall. Truly important people like newsreaders mingled with politicians, media executives, agents and publicists.

At the A P Watt table, tension was rising. Kirk had consumed a fair amount of alcohol and was starting to behave erratically. He was dressed as Lord Byron in a black velvet suit and flamboyant, frilly white silk shirt. On their way to their seats, passing a collection of politically correct social celebrities, a toothy cockney female called Janet had shrieked to her companions, a fat, failed pop star and an elderly charity worker who had become a successful television millionaire, 'Ooh look, Bob and Paul, it's that Elizabeth Regeeena!'

To which Kirk had commented under his breath, yet quite loudly enough to be heard, 'That's Regina — as in the place you talk out of, Madam.'

He found the artificial, phony, 'luvvie' atmosphere quite unpleasant and unsettling and drank several more glasses of wine to compensate. They had passed Venom, tucked away on a table at the back, half-concealed behind a pillar, and his expression of friendly delight had looked as phony as it indeed was.

Kirk had spotted a good-looking young waiter of 18 serving tables, refreshing water glasses and brushing away crumbs, tall and blond with button nose and a perfect, peach-tinted, hairless complexion and had become convinced that the boy found him wildly attractive.

'He keeps staring at me,' he whispered to Elizabeth.

'What do you expect?' she hissed back. 'You're not exactly ordinary Booker guest material.'

The young man, working part-time with his father who held a more senior job with the catering company, was indeed transfixed by the sight of the strange, grotesque, little creature.

The excitement grew and the Chairman rose to announce the winner and begin a lengthy and rather noble speech, aimed directly at the voters. It was clear that he intended to continue for some time. He discussed the literary state of schools and universities and praised the encouragement by government of education in colleges. Several media pundits loudly and blatantly yawned without attempting to cover their mouths. Unperturbed, Partigan continued. His voice soared up the tall columns and was lost in the vast space above, echoey vowels and mashed consonants hissing into the darkness of history.

Kirk decided to go to the toilet but changed direction with a flurry of crutches when he saw the handsome waiter passing through some service doors. On the other side, he discovered that they were alone in a cleaning area. Clearly convinced by the boy's startled, terrified look that he was indeed fancied, in one move he unzipped his trousers and pulled out his very erect and quite substantial circumcised cock.

The reaction was suitably impressive. Letting out a shriek, the youth dropped his tray with a resounding crash and rushed back out through the swing doors. Popping his dick back inside his pants, Kirk followed him to apologise. He was half-way across the floor when the boy's father, in receipt of his son's hysterical account, charged at him.

At this moment, Hartley Partigan MP reached his climax and announced, '... and the winner is ... Leslie Prince for *Ramadan Mislaid*!'

As Elizabeth Regina stood up to wild applause and astonishment, the man's fist smacked Kirk under his chin, lifting his body into the air and depositing him with a crash on the centre of the minor celebrities' table.

Cutlery, crockery, food, wine, glasses, cups and coffee flew in every direction. Guests sprang to their feet and fell over backwards. Janet began swearing uncontrollably. Kirk struggled to regain his position and the table collapsed under his weight. Mustard splattered the failed pop star. Elizabeth, who had started towards the rostrum to accept the award, ready to reveal her alter ego, changed course towards her friend at top speed, bowling over several shocked diners. Other staff restrained the assailant and rushed him out to the kitchen areas. Panic, pandemonium and chaos ensued.

BBC lenses were zooming all over the place, the director undecided whether or not to capture the disturbance at the same time as trying to spot Leslie Prince. His PA was shouting, 'It's the cripple! I'm sure it's the cripple!' The producer was yelling, 'Cut away; go to the judges; focus on Partigan ...' The experts had given up all pretence at cool and were jamming their noses against the glass, peering at the drama. Unfortunately, they were momentarily caught in this uncomfortable position by one of the random camera feeds. Most of the diners had abandoned their coffee and had risen to their feet, anxiously standing on tip-toe to watch the fiasco over other guests' heads.

As Elizabeth realised that her big moment was ruined, she started to see the funny side and began giggling uncontrollably. Still, having ascertained that Kirk was all right, she diverted back to the podium at the top table, grabbed the microphone and spoke.

'Thank you for this honour. I am Leslie Prince. I am also Elizabeth Regina. Both are pseudonyms. The man lying on the floor over there, flapping like a landed trout, was the inspiration for *Ramadan Mislaid* and is also my boyfriend. We are hoping to get married. If we've ruined the dignity of this event, I apologise. But believe me, it's been fun!'

She then had to sit down because she was laughing so much.

It was not a standard acceptance speech.

Eighteen

*L*isa Littlejohn had truly proven her mettle for all time.

Upon witnessing the débâcle, she had immediately followed Kirk's assailant out into the kitchen and was swiftly smoothing away his complaints with dedicated diplomacy.

A lot was made of bad publicity, embarrassing consequences, upset employers, damaging career effects and assault charges. Confronted by this elegant, reasonable woman in smart twin set and pearls, the man was soothed and persuaded to leave for home with his son, no harm done, let's forget the entire episode.

By the time the media investigators had arrived, the offending situation had been spirited away and substituted with a tale of too much alcohol consumed and trivial insults delivered. No longer a story. Nobody noticed the shadowy figure with pock-marked skin who watched and listened and observed.

Such talents, far away and above the norm for an agent and usually sadly lacking in the finest publicist, won Lisa the Teaser a permanent spot in both Elizabeth and Kirk's hearts.

Kirk, meanwhile, had been quietly removed from the Guildhall to the safe regions of their hotel whilst Elizabeth was accepting accolades and doing the promised BBC television live and exclusive interview.

'What inspired you to write such a very different novel?'

'As I said, it was meeting Kirk Kurabbi and his friends in Tangier on holiday a few months ago. I decided to publish under a pseudonym because I'm so well known for the very successful romances I compose under the name Elizabeth Regina that I felt serious critics would not come to it unaccompanied by baggage.'

It was the first of many virtually identical question and answer sessions.

Later, safely back in Willings, she asked Kirk what on earth had happened.

'Well, I got rather drunk, became convinced that boy fancied me, followed him into the kitchen and showed him my weapon. Clearly, he changed his mind as soon as he saw it!'

There was never any attempt at concealment with Kirk.

'Do you think you could try to avoid such behaviour when we're married?'

'I can't guarantee that, old girl. Alcohol brings out my former urges. But I will try to consider the consequences.'

Under the circumstances, she felt that was the best she could hope for.

Now everything was out in the open, they agreed that a wedding would be a good idea sooner rather than later. Neither had the slightest doubt about the wisdom of the move.

'It makes little or no sense logically,' said Kirk, 'but we happen to be in love with each other, unlikely though that may seem to everybody else, and even to our own more sensible considerations, but since it's the case, we might as well get on with it and make it official.'

They decided to celebrate in the ancient church in the nearby village of Forest Green, a quaint and miniature edifice with tiny grounds and ivy-covered walls. Eddie, Maria and Jock were invited to represent Kirk's family. There was plenty of room for them to stay at Willings. Elizabeth tactfully provided them with first-class round-trip GB Air tickets.

The packing and preparation in Tangier was extensive. The bars and the beach were tenderly placed in the temporary hands of trusted friends. Gifts were purchased after serious bargaining. There were tears and messages, scribbled notes and lengthy farewells. Even Frau Meisel sucked in her cheeks, diluted her bitchiness and resisted spitting venom as she sent fond congratulations in German.

The Terrible Threesome, as Elizabeth fondly nicknamed them, arrived at Willings looking like caricature visitors from an illustrated children's book about eccentrics.

Maria had put on far too much mascara and lipstick in an attempt to appear respectable and British, much of which had smudged, giving her the facial aspect of Lila Kedrova in the movie *Zorba the Greek*.

Edward Vere, not at all at home in his country of origin, was wrapped and protected from the elements in a very elderly Burberry raincoat, which he considered fashionable, and a moth-eaten cashmere scarf, which he described as warm. The result, however, was to make him resemble a wino from Waterloo.

Jock, who had decided that such an occasion required full regalia, wore kilt, sporran, tartan, beret and had only just been dissuaded from carrying bagpipes.

Their physical appearance did not matter, however, for the warmth of their greeting made both Kirk and Elizabeth rather tearful. Much embracing and cuddling took place.

And they passed the ultimate test. The spaniels instantly took to each of them and gambolled around with quite uncontrollable joy.

Maria was the most impressed by the old house and insisted on examining every single nook and cranny. She found several nooks but not a single cranny.

She pored over old documents and detailed evidence of the history of Willings, fascinated by every owner and tenant, and the high spot of her visit was when she discovered a patch of strange, unknown weeds in a corner of the garden which she took to be positive proof that one of the earliest dwellers had been a herbalist. And very swiftly she deserted her attempts to be a glamorous country lady and happily crammed her considerable charms into jeans, jumpers, woolly overcoats and wellington boots.

Eddie and Jock joined Kirk on his paddock walks with the spaniels. They were so enamoured by the atmosphere that their customary consumption of Scotch was reduced alarmingly. They sat for many happy hours beside the roaring, blazing hearth and nursed a tumbler, often forgetting to refill it.

A year ago, Elizabeth would never in her wildest dreams have imagined hosting this foursome at Willings. But she could not have been happier in their company.

Nineteen

The pub dining-room served extremely bad Indian food, which did nothing to improve Venom's halitosis. Puffing vindaloo and germs at the Editor of the *News of the World*, HRH was getting into his stride.

'I have evidence of serious fraud by their closest friend, a stockbroker called Lewis McKenzie, which will make bondwashing seem like casual laundry. And their sick relationship involves devil worship, small children and ...' he lowered his voice, not wanting to shock, '... dogs!'

It was the culmination of months of planning. He'd prised contacts out of his seedier acquaintances, wined and dined assistant features editors, shown them examples of his lengthy investigations, inflated facts and embellished insinuations.

He'd been in more nasty bars and grubby

cafés than he'd ever imagined existed. They seemed to be the meeting places of choice for the hacks stuck amongst the run-down dockland renovations.

The Editor of the *News of the World* was not overly impressed by Henry and his dreadful complexion. She was trying to juggle a highly pressurised job and a complicated personal life, something which became more difficult by the day.

But her Features Editor was right. This was a good story. The man had the facts. He had pictures, sneaked at unflattering moments a year earlier in Maria's bar.

She knew he was a shit but it wouldn't be the first time she had slipped into bed with a shit, metaphorically, of course. No — not just metaphorically. Her time as Secretary to the Editor of *The Times* had involved her in behaviour she'd never allow on to the pages of her current organ.

It wasn't easy being a career woman. It was still a man's world, no matter how the politically correct pretended. Oh, the hypocrisy! That was the key, wasn't it? Hypocrisy. Pretend to be shocked and horrified, display righteous indignation at activities everybody would love to indulge in and, since they themselves had no prospects of getting anywhere close, chose to condemn with horror.

Venom's novel had died the proverbial

death. Reviews had been ghastly and sales even worse. He was no longer regarded as an important writer and he'd never been a commercial one.

The bitterness had turned his already bilious stomach acids into lethal liquid. Desperate to do damage and keen to boost his empty bank balance, he'd collected his snaps and exaggerated his stories, copied the stolen documents and sworn affidavits.

He wanted an awful lot of money ('broke ... I'm afraid, last book didn't sell too well ...') but the increased circulation could warrant the expense.

'Payment on publication only,' she stated.

'No problem.'

'Let's go through it once again,' she said wearily, wondering why this migraine never went away.

*　　　*　　　*

Both Eddie and Jock had totally abandoned their distant British relatives years ago, most of whom had passed away in any case, but Maria had kept in touch with her family and was determined to visit them.

She seriously wanted her friends to come with her. Kirk was nervous, since he anticipated it could lead to an unfortunate encounter with his own relations, but Elizabeth convinced him that it would be better to confront such situations at this time.

'It's the only area that's confusing you in your life. Why not put it behind you whilst you've got both me and The Terrible Threesome to back you up and give you moral support?' she said.

So, one morning, they set off. Shortly after leaving Willings, the weather grew ominous. At first, big drops of rain splattered against the windscreen. Then it turned into a torrent and the journey was long and slow, wipers thrashing and tidal waves gushing in their wake. Just as they reached Yorkshire, the clouds passed as rapidly as they had arrived and the sun came out. Rich, green and wet, the trees and shrubs looked stunning. Maria was quite overcome by her memories.

After the initial coldness all those years ago, her family, unlike that of Kirk's mother, had forgiven her and welcomed her back emotionally into their arms, so she had kept in touch, through letters and calls, but she hadn't visited in over a decade.

Her parents were still alive, crumbly, wrinkly, decrepit Northerners, bent and aching, short-sighted and dour, living day to day with memories of the distant past. They had no passion with which to welcome her, but they made the visitors tea and scones.

Father and mother, peas in the pod, living

waxworks, dry of skin and more parched still in vocabulary. Little to say, less to feel.

Without immediate siblings, the rest of Maria's clan were aunts and uncles and cousins. They were friendly enough to total strangers, though clearly taken aback by the unusual Kirk.

Kirk's grandparents were both dead. His own uncles and aunts would have allowed him access, if churlishly, but circumstances meant they were occupied elsewhere. Maria's family had lost touch with most of them anyway. One second cousin arrived at the house to peer at her long-lost legendary relation, shared a mug of warm tea and left after nodding and grinning nervously.

The nephew and family who now lived in his mother's old home expressed no interest in coming over and were otherwise involved and unable therefore to invite him to visit them. The vague prospect of such words as 'will' and 'inheritance' clearly provoked their disinclination.

Both Maria and Kirk felt rather empty as they drove silently back to Surrey. It had been a disappointing trip for both of them. Maria had discovered that time, as well as being the great healer, was also capable of moving events forward so inevitably that the world totally, if gradually, changed. And Kirk, having harboured resentment for his whole life, had found that the objects of his hatred had virtually no interest in him whatsoever. And now neither did he in them.

Their dinner was subdued. Their friends realised that false merriment was not required. Understanding gentle peace was the best atmosphere.

*   *   *

The phone rang.

'Relax,' Kirk said to Elizabeth, who was exhausted. 'I'll deal with it. You go upstairs and lie down.'

*   *   *

Elizabeth had booked a vast tent to be erected in the Willings garden for the reception after the ceremony and Lewis McKenzie's vivacious wife Bridget, an expert in catering and decoration, had taken charge of ensuring that both food and atmosphere would be memorable. Eddie had been selected by Kirk as his Best Man. Maria, of course, was giving him away. Lisa and Isobella were the Bridesmaids or, as Isobella preferred to be described, the Ladies in Waiting. The vicar, a garrulous, myopic gentleman with wispy grey hair and a clucking wife, had read the banns and met the bridegroom (Elizabeth felt that, under the circumstances, this was rather important).

It seemed that Elizabeth's fiancé had an

uncanny and natural ability when it came to stocks and shares.

This gave her more pleasure than almost anything else. Kirk could stand alone, not needing to rely on her income, capable of building his own career through his own skills and brains. Self-esteem would be a vital ingredient in their life together.

But for a few days Kirk was strangely quiet, almost brooding. He went quietly to London several times on his own. Elizabeth didn't question him. She knew he was coping with the emotions aroused by his voyage north.

Meanwhile, her own status was continuing to rise. The expected backlash against *Ramadan Mislaid* had not materialised. Nearly every Booker Prize winner suffered a subsequent critical reaction but respected reviewers were still raving about the novel, of which sales were soaring. Indeed, they were reaching the dizzy heights of her Regina page-turners. Hodder Headline were absolutely delighted.

And the BBC had been pleased by the response to the unusual coverage of the event. Much discussion and reshowing of excerpts had resulted, guaranteeing massive ratings for future stagings. Still, nobody had quite ascertained why the row had exploded, but it was considered damn fine television.

The wedding was scheduled for the following Saturday afternoon. Guests had been invited. Inflatable marquees were erected. Servants and chefs employed and trained. Costumes and finery acquired and fitted. Eddie had the ring, which he kept checking was safe in his pocket. The Moroccan Ambassador and his wife had accepted an invitation, as had several very helpful Foreign Office mandarins. The spaniels had been informed they were not to come to church but could attend the reception. The weather was predicted to be fine. Nothing appeared to be destined to go wrong.

But Kirk and Elizabeth, in bed the night before, were keeping their fingers firmly crossed. They were well aware of the possibilities.

Twenty

As it happened, Sod's Law came into force and it all went wonderfully.

Elizabeth looked quite gorgeous in her striking wedding gown, a mass of tulle and lace and woven gold and silver threads and precious stones. Love had enhanced her. She had lost a little weight and was trim, vibrant and glowing. Kirk, too, managed to strike a splendid figure, smart and handsome, helped by the fact that he was enjoying himself so much that he spent the entire day smiling and it has already been noted that a beaming Kirk was a very attractive creature indeed.

The weather was perfect. Delightful sunshine, clear blue sky, no breeze at all. Hundreds of thousands of flowers; banks of petals; the incredible scent of a million bouquets.

The service proceeded like clockwork. Eddie did not lose the ring; nobody fainted or spoke out against the union; the priest never fluffed a line; and there was absolutely no bad behaviour from anybody, especially the groom. The church looked like a dream, with tall, stained-glass windows, spire, quaint crooked gate and path, wooden pews and an octogenarian organist.

The reception was a major triumph. Bridget McKenzie, sparkling and electric as her red hair tumbled to her shoulders, conducted the proceedings like a maestro. The food was delicious, caviar and quails' eggs, *foie gras* and smoked salmon, grilled spare ribs and sliced veal with cream and mushrooms and, the speciality surprise, *raie au beurre noir*, courtesy of a rather secret recipe provided by Maria.

Champagne flowed. There was Puligny Montrachet and Château Latour. There were clarets and liqueurs, tea and coffee. The conversations were polite yet interesting, formal and fond.

There was a string quartet of priceless ability performing the works of Mozart and Beethoven with grace and subtlety. Politicians mixed with literary figures and the kind of minor celebrities that had so poisoned the Booker ceremony were totally absent. Only the very nicest guests had been invited.

Maria and Kirk got into a very positive dialogue with the Moroccan Ambassador and his wife which looked likely to lead to most important benefits on their return to Tangier. The

Ambassador was a cultured man, educated at Eton and Oxford and closely related by his marriage to the Moroccan Royal Family. Both Kirk and Elizabeth had agreed that they would buy a small house in Tangier as well as living at Willings. The combination of both environments seemed ideal to the two of them. The Ambassador knew of a delightful mansion on the outskirts of town which looked just like Tara from *Gone with the Wind*; indeed, it had been expressly designed for a film-lover to be virtually identical to Brett and Scarlet's legendary pad. It had apparently been up for sale for a couple of years, since the owner's boyfriend had tragically died young, but was rather too expensive for most Moroccans. Ideal, however, as a holiday home for wealthy Europeans. Contacts were passed across.

The spaniels became seriously overfed with titbits, stopped begging for scraps, found warm spots under tables far from insensitive feet and decided that sleep was a most preferable option.

Lisa the Teaser hit it off with Jock and they spent hours chattering about the world. The urban sophisticate and the ex-patriot Glaswegian discovered vast tracts of mutual interest. The others were amazed by the relationship. In many ways, they could not have been more different. Kirk made Elizabeth laugh by suggesting that Lisa's work with various writers meant she was probably the only human being who could actually understand what Jock was saying! Isobella and Eddie were comparing experiences. Marriage for a start. Isobella had done it many times; Eddie had managed to avoid it. She talked of how it had never worked. He told her it was because she did it for all the wrong reasons. 'Only love,' said Eddie wisely, pointing at the bride and groom. And Isobella, normally so dim though so sweet, had looked at him with fresh sight. The hundreds of other guests gobbled grub and quenched their thirst with abandon.

As the day finished and the newlyweds were left to their own devices, except for the army of servants and contractors cleaning up the debris, Kirk and Elizabeth went upstairs and lay down relaxing.

'So — I suppose I'm Mrs Kurabbi now.'

'Better than Miss Smith,' he smiled, 'and far superior to Ms Regina or Mr Prince!'

He stroked her with his fingertips. 'I never thought all this would happen,' he said. 'Although everything felt great at the time, I just expected it to last as long as you were in Tangier. Then you brought me over, and I treated that as a surprise extra perk. But slowly it became clear we genuinely regarded each other in the same way and now, here we are, man and wife.'

'So how does it feel now?'

'Unbelievable. Everything I ever dreamed about. Someone who loves me and cares about me. Someone I feel the same way about. A home.

A family. Even, dare I say it, the possibility of a career. Yet, just a few months ago, I hadn't the vaguest conception that it could happen.'

'Don't worry. It's just as strange for me. Fifty-one years of standard behaviour. I thought all my values and barriers were set in concrete. My mind was totally closed to any changes. I was doing very well and coping with a single life. My mind had shut out all the aspects I'd missed out on and I'd decided I didn't want them anyway. Then everything turned upside-down. And I've never known happiness like this. Love. Marriage to a man half my age. Critical praise after years of scribbling pop pulp. It's as though I've been blessed.'

One of the dogs jumped up on to the bed and snuffled up to them affectionately, cool, wet, black nose; floppy pink tongue; golden fur and loving eyes.

'Are you really content and happy? Truly certain that nothing could divide us?'

She looked at him quizzically. 'That sounds like trouble.'

'Could be,' said Kirk. 'A few weeks ago I got a tip-off that Venom had sold a really scurrilous story to the *News of the World*. Not only was it intended to ruin us, he'd found some documents when he rifled through Lewis' desk when we were there all those months ago and he intended to bring him down, too.'

Elizabeth shot bolt upright, a chill shattering

her wellbeing.

'I decided to take the bull by the horns. Instead of telling you, I went up there and walked into the Editor's office myself. Well, I use the word "walked" loosely.'

'I put all the cards on the table. I told her the truth about myself. I said I was prepared to give them my story in every detail gratis, free, for nothing. In return, they should drop Venom and I pointed out that his assessment of the McKenzie document was not only inaccurate but dangerously libellous. I detailed and explained it and, when I produced a page that had clearly been intentionally omitted by Venom, she immediately saw the truth. She was, of course, delighted to get a story for which she was poised to pay thousands for free, as well as being relieved to escape the inevitable expensive law suit. I even convinced her that Venom had also intentionally concealed various sheets of figures which proved Lewis' activities to be totally legal. But, I'm afraid, although, she agreed to postpone carrying the story until we were married, it runs tomorrow. We'd better be prepared for all hell to break loose.'

Twenty-One

To everybody's relief, the story was nowhere near as bad as it might have been.

Even editors are human and Kirk's charm had converted another fan.

It was lurid and colourful, but good journalists have a way of writing that can take the sting out of a story just as easily as they can put one in. There were loud headlines and sordid expressions but most of their friends felt it was a damp squib. The big loser of the episode was Venom. The paper carried several exposés about him which were framed in a much nastier style. He received no payment. Karma strikes again.

Even the Guildhall episode, whilst including the funnier parts of the story, omitted the more disgraceful elements. Kirk was rather disappointed.

'They could have made me much more

disgusting,' he complained.

'How did you get hold of the document that proved Lewis's innocence?' asked Elizabeth. 'Does he know what you did?'

'I have a very good eye for detail and quite a memory for fonts and graphics,' smiled Kirk, who had become extremely computer literate. 'Put it this way — if all else collapses, I've got a future career as a forger! And no, he has no idea. I'd prefer it to stay that way. I didn't do it to get any favours.'

*   *   *

'So what are your plans? Another Regina novel? A Leslie Prince sequel — *Ramadan Regained*, perhaps?'

Lisa was joking but there was a serious purpose to her question. Could Elizabeth go back to the highly lucrative, if creatively unsatifying, construction of frothy romances or was she now hooked on the praise and prestige of critically acclaimed works?

'The answer is — I'd like to have my cake and eat it. Haven't you often thought that a ridiculous metaphor? What's the point of having your cake and not eating it? But the way *Ramadan Mislaid* is selling, there seems to be no reason why I can't write another novel that's both good and commercial. I think I'd like to try that first, before banging out another Regina page-turner. But I'm not against doing both. The old romances mean more now — after all, I've got personal experience at last!'

'How's married life?'

'Fantastic. We agreed that Kirk should keep his own rooms and private areas and he's developing a tremendous ability in the investment area — Lewis feels he's a natural. The way it's going, he'll be keeping me in the style to which I've become accustomed. We're happy to be with each other, but already we're building lives that can exist apart, so there's no pressure, only pleasure.'

'If you do another Leslie Prince, will you continue the Islamic theme?'

'No, I don't think so. I'd like to cover a totally different subject. Kirk was my inspiration for the first book. He'll still be my guiding light but it would be wrong to use his experiences again. No — the next Prince book will be as unlike the first as that was to the Regina series. But I've also had some ideas to take forward the essential joy of the first book — the fun, the anarchic element, the surprise. I think it broke down barriers and made people rethink their prejudices.'

'You can say that again. Look at me and Jock!'

'Yes, I've been wanting to ask you about that. What on earth have an elderly, grizzled Tangerine bar owner and an elegant, sophisticated, West End agent got in common?'

'Coming from you, that's cheek!'

They laughed.

*   *   *

They were sitting outside in deck chairs, sipping freshly squeezed lemonade and enjoying the early summer sunshine. Elizabeth sat up and spluttered.

'How are you feeling? You look a little peaky.'

'Yes,' replied Elizabeth, 'it's this ridiculous cold. I can't seem to shake it off. It started as a mere snuffle which got more and more bunged up until I was having problems sleeping. Then it went to my throat and I almost lost my voice and now it's on my chest. I keep retching up chunks of green plastic.'

'Ugh! Charming. Nowhere near me, if you don't mind!'

Indeed, Elizabeth was paler than she should have been and distinctly wheezy, with dark circles under her eyes. When she had a fit of coughing, it turned into an asthmatic hiss; a dry rattle that sounded very unhealthy.

'The trouble with colds at this time of year is that you resent them more than when the weather is filthy and chilly and damp. At least then you feel you deserve it. Staying in bed is a sort of pleasure — all wrapped up warm taking

Night Nurse while the winter howls outside and you've got a hot toddy and some pillows cuddled around you. But now you feel stupid even staying inside, when there's this gorgeous, cloudless, sunny paradise to sit out in.'

Kirk kept telling her that she wouldn't get better unless she went to bed and allowed herself to be pampered by him and the servants until she recovered completely. That night, after Lisa had returned to town, Elizabeth decided to do as her husband insisted and retired to her sick chamber.

But the infection stuck to her lungs and would not disperse. Her local GP came over several times, prescribing antibiotics and decongestants to no avail. After a few days he started getting worried.

'I think it's in danger of turning into pneumonia and you ought to go into hospital,' he said.

With Kirk's support, she agreed and they drove her to the local clinic. Small, cosy and compact, it had a pleasant atmosphere, charming nurses and some very good doctors.

But, after various tests and analyses, she seemed to get no better. Her lungs felt on fire. She was wheezing and clearing her throat and was feverish and bunged up. She could not sleep. She tossed and sweated. Kirk hardly left her bedside. Whenever she woke, he was there to fetch her a drink of water. Her appetite disappeared. She started hallucinating. Hot and cold; perspiring in buckets; limbs like lead weights; headaches; swollen glands. The nurses were angels, checking her continually. Eventually, with much care and constant monitoring, she turned the corner. Her chest cleared up, she began to breathe more easily again and, though exhausted, she was clearly on the mend.

For some days, her recuperation continued. Slowly she'd get better, then slip back again, then revive again. After a while it became a regular improvement. Everybody heaved a sigh of relief. It had been touch and go.

Lying pale and drawn in her hospital bed one morning, strong enough to sip some tea, Kirk and the specialist came and sat at the foot of her bed in her little private room.

'What on earth was that all about?' she asked. 'Is there some kind of terminal 'flu going round? That totally wiped me out — and I thought it was just another three-day cold.'

Kirk and the doctor looked at each other and the medical man cleared his throat.

'You seem much better and your husband said he thought you'd prefer to be told the truth when you were strong enough to cope,' he said. 'The fact of the matter is — you have developed full-blown AIDS.'

Twenty-Two

*I*t doesn't seem fair.

Just a couple of years to live, at most, and I've only found real happiness in the past few months.

The worst thing of all is that the very cause of my happiness has been the probable cause of my death.

Without one, I'd not have the other.

Kirk is being eaten up with shame, guilt and fear — he's HIV positive, of course, so it's a death sentence for him, too, but it's my situation that's causing him the most pain. He keeps saying, over and over again, that he'll never forgive himself. That he deserves his own problems but that I don't deserve anything.

I point out that his love has brought me the greatest joy in my life. That's much more important than the negative ramifications.

I'm trying to be positive about it. I've told myself

not to be stupid. We all die eventually. Some through an unforeseen accident. Others after a long and agonising illness. There's actually a bonus in knowing when you're going. You can appreciate the final years much more. I could have discovered cancer and been through months of radiation, chemotherapy and still died at the end of it. I could have been run over by a bus and lost the use of various limbs, been blinded, paralysed, comatose. Anyway, I should count my blessings. Fifty-two years of a generally enjoyable and healthy life crowned with tremendous luck at the end. But the sensible words have a way of not reaching the heart and I still find myself overwhelmed by depression.

I'm not in pain and the specialists say there's no reason why, if I take care of myself, I can't survive for some time without serious illness. But I'm incredibly tired and totally lacking in energy. I keep trying to write but composing this letter alone, dear Lisa, is exhausting me.

I'm determined to conquer this pessimistic lethargy. I would like to produce at least one more novel of the standard of Ramadan Mislaid. Quite apart from anything else, two books is a safer legacy than one. Those critics can dismiss a lucky fluke, but you get your place in history after a couple of classics.

But every day I wake with a heavy hand on my shoulders. 'Closer to the grave,' whispers a voice in my ear. How ridiculous. Every morning we are all closer to death. Memento Mori. Yet the certainty that there's not long, enjoy it while you can, make the best of your final months, concentrates the mind in a gloomy, resentful, tiring, negative way.

I think my greatest regret is that I didn't find this happiness sooner so that I'd have had longer to cherish it. But then I remember that the cause came with the gift. Probably both at exactly the same second, in that hotel bedroom in Tangier. I changed totally at that moment, in every conceivable way. More than I realised, and that was a lot.

When I walk around, seeing the places and things I most love, I feel peaceful, yet robbed. It's as though I was given the most beautiful prize and had it snatched away instantly, without a hope of getting it back.

It hasn't affected my feelings for Kirk. I still see him with love, hold him, want him, need him. But I can sense his fury. Not against me. Not against whoever gave it to him. But against himself.

How can I ease that self-loathing? I keep telling him not to blame himself. I keep reminding him that I'd have paid any price to have experienced what we have together. Yes — including death. If given the chance again now, with all the information available, I'd have done the same. The plus is far greater than the minus.

But that's too logical. It's the brain talking, not the soul.

My soul is aching, hurting, resenting. It's furious, grieving, despising, tossing and turning. If there was a God, I'd ask him what to do. I'd beg him or her for their help in coping with this agony. Not to *withstand the inevitable physical pain, not even to give my spirit peace and quiet. No — if there was one thing I'd ask, it would be to make Kirk forgive himself.*

Any ideas, girl? You've always been the one to come up with the clever solutions. That first dodgy deal with Hodder Headline, that went on to make us and them millions. Your cunning clauses in the Leslie Prince contract. And we'll never forget your instant PR job the night of the Booker Prize ceremony. So how about it? Put your thinking cap on and come up with some way for me to comfort my man.

Lots of love from my (metaphorical) sick bed,

Your friend,

Elizabeth

*　　　　*　　　　*

It's not fair.

All she did was fall in love with me. Now, as a direct result, she's dying. And I'm having to watch. She's thin and pale and depressed and, worst of all, trying to put a brave face on it.

I never thought it would be possible to be purged of bitterness and anger at my physical state. But suddenly I forgot my birthright. More — I rejoiced in it. Because that's what attracted her to me. She'd probably have been bored to tears if I'd been a handsome, dull Arab stud, fully in control of my body.

She was interested in me and then she determined to write about me and slowly she fell in love with me. And I thought she was just another tourist to be pleasantly ripped off for a few drinks, some food, entertainment and, possibly, hard cash. But it's amazing how exhilarating it can be when someone is clearly fascinated by you. As she learned more, she started to care and began to like me. And I warmed to her. I was amused by her questions, intrigued by her curiosity and flattered by her appreciation. She was no sylphlike goddess, slender and delicious, gorgeous, pouting, a siren of sexuality. She was a middle-aged, decent, plump, bright, sensitive, funny, astute and intelligent mature woman. Not the ideal beach partner if I'd cared about what observers were thinking. Not the sort of bimbo to hook on to your arm and make your peers seethe with envy. But a stimulating friend. And I started to find her attractive, too. Then it happened.

It should never have happened but it did, and now I feel myself wishing I'd contrived it, planned it, seduced her, made her fall for me in order to achieve selfish goals. Then, now I could truly, justifiably hate myself. I would have been rent-a-demon. Like a predator, spotting my victim, coldly calculating her bank balance, loneliness, vulnerability, potential. I would have pounced, slowly and cunningly, and dragged her foolish into my web like a killer spider with a fat fly. That sort of reprehensible behaviour would have validated my punishment.

But I was as innocent as she was. And as honest. We fell for each other simultaneously. There was no wickedness or evil or dishonesty or selfishness. Two totally opposite people, cynical about the world, not prepared to be taken advantage of, tuned into the fake and phony elements of life, ruthless in our protection of our privacy, not prepared to get involved, impossible to trick, conscious of the traps. Which is why this is so unfair. Surely, neither of us has deserved this?

But especially not her. So my mission in life is to make every second of the rest of her life a joy. To give her every ounce of love and pleasure and care that it's possible to provide. To cram a decade into every month and a week into each hour. To amuse her and entertain her and charm her and surprise her and cherish her and please her and show her the best of humanity. I'm going to dig deep inside myself and find the most positive, truest qualities. Let's be honest; I've not got that long myself. So I'll become the best I can be.

The first thing is to destroy this bitterness. Fate could have struck many other ways. I'd be dying if I'd never met her, and without the incredible happiness she brought me. Look at it as a blessing. Personally, I'm way better off than if I'd never set eyes on her. My poor body was infected years ago; God knows how — there were so many possible routes. But that's why it's so hard for me not to resent the situation. Elizabeth brought me nothing but joy and I've killed her.

But I must convince her I'm not blaming myself all the time because I'm well aware that her greatest depression is caused by my own self-condemnation. Get it together, Kirk, and put on a smiling face which reflects inner peace.

She's too astute to hoodwink, though. I've got to banish that guilt truly. I can't fool her. If she senses I've truly come to terms with this tragic turn of events, she'll be able to find her own acceptance.

It's going to be the hardest task I've ever confronted but I'll do it.

*   *   *

Odd creatures these humans.

They think *we're* odd. All we ever want to do is eat, go walkies and be made a fuss of.

Yet that's all they want to do, too.

She goes walkies every hour or so these days. She finds it very soothing and relaxing. Like the others, she pretends that the shouts and cries and calls are for me to come and seek and find but actually they are so automatic and natural that they calm her mind. Self-hypnosis really. I pretend to obey but I know why she's doing it. It's for herself, not for me. That's fine. That's what I'm here for. And she's sad. I can feel it in her fingers as she strokes me. Wonderful that. Soothing and calming for both of us. But you get to know what she is thinking. And she's definitely sad at the moment. Her fingertips convey memories and dreams and nostalgia and wishes of what might have been.

I just wiggle and nuzzle and try to make her feel better. It seems to work. Every time I make a fuss of her she perks up.

It doesn't matter if it's raining when we go walkies, because then she has to pull on boots and dry my paws afterwards, which does her good, too. I get as muddy as possible. That's what she likes. Keeps her occupied. And, if it's hot and dry and dusty, then I make sure I've collected loads of burrs and tangle and weed and she'll scold me as she brushes and scrapes and polishes me until my fur shines golden and burnished and she feels truly fine.

She's much thinner than she used to be. Ought to eat a bit more, fatten herself up. Can't be good for her, this skinniness. She was quite heavy but now she's just skin and bones. She needs the food for energy, like I do, but you can't tell a woman anything.

Gets sick a lot, too. I try to go into the bathroom and nuzzle her and cheer her up but she doesn't want to know when she's being ill. Pushes me away. Makes a horrid noise and an even worse smell and cries a lot.

Then she comes back out and lies down on her bed and after a while she wants me back and I jump up and curl close to her and she starts stroking me again and then she feels better.

The man is being very good to us. I can feel his love, too, and he's trying hard for her. He's always cared. I liked him from the start. He's patient and soft and good. Walks strange but gets there in the end, which is what counts after all. Every moment he's there with her if she needs him but waits quietly on his own if she's ill or sleeping. Then he likes me to go and visit him and he strokes me, too.

Big hands, strong wrists, powerful and affectionate. Hour after hour, gently rubbing my fur. He's an ear man — you know, kneading and tugging, scratching and pulling, whereas she's a chest girl, always manipulating and tickling, deep into that sensitive area just below the neck. Both very satisfying actually. She finds it makes her pleasantly drowsy. He needs it even more than she does and I try to help by showing him how much I love him, too.

Humans are most peculiar; one moment up, the next down. I'm always the same, never changing. It makes life much easier. Walkies ... food ... sleepies. Quite simple.

I often think they don't really appreciate us.

After all, we make it so natural to them, so intuitive, so instinctive that they don't think about the relaxing qualities of owning a dog. But then we wouldn't be any use if they thought about it. They should just allow us to be a vital but unassuming part of their leisure. When we do crop up in their consciousness, they think they are looking after us. Feeding us, exercising us, combing and brushing us. Sweet, isn't it?

But they are definitely going through some kind of stress at the moment. Which is when I can be the most help. In gratitude for those thousands of Bonios and Chocolate Titbits and those hours of throwing sticks and wrestling with squeaky balls and chewy frisbees, it's the least I can do. Peace of mind is what they are looking for. And that's exactly what I can help them find.

Twenty-Three

TOP WRITER DYING OF AIDS!

The surprise, highly acclaimed winner of the Booker Prize this year is dying of AIDS.

Elizabeth Regina, the huge-selling novelist of romantic stories that, for years, have been a prime addiction for bored housewives, was revealed last month to be the real person behind the pseudonym Leslie Prince, writer of *Ramadan Mislaid*, the runaway champion of the Booker contest, the Oscars of the literary world.

The prim, polite, proper middle-aged lady attributed her inspiration to young Arab Kirk Kurabbi, a paraplegic Moroccan of 25 with an English mother, whom Regina met on vacation in Tangier. His character formed the basis for the hero of her critically-praised bestseller.

Astonishingly, Kirk and Elizabeth also fell in

love and they married — a spring/autumn romance which could have come straight from the pages of one of her earlier Regina page-turners. The ceremony was a delightful occasion in an 'olde worlde' country chapel. *Hello!* magazine did a spread on the event. Great joy lit up the rolling green hills of the Surrey countryside.

But, sadly, there is not to be a happy ending to this story. Last month she fell sick and was diagnosed as suffering from AIDS. Now she is a bed-ridden invalid in Willings, her country mansion, being cared for by her husband, rapidly deteriorating as he pines with misery.

The story behind this tragedy involves the sleazy, dope-ridden world of underground Morocco. The bars of Tangier have long been a breeding ground for sick perversion and drug addiction. Western tourists flock there for sex holidays. Stimulants of every kind are freely available. Ex-hippies and deported criminals survive by catering to the most vile secret lusts. Crack cocaine, heroin, under-age children sold for abuse, marijuana and black-market money are freely bargained alongside the carpets and coffee in the filthy tunnels of the casbah. And it was as a part of this cesspool of vermin that Kirk Kurabbi survived.

Somehow, his adventures made him contract the HIV virus which this newspaper has exclusively learned was the source of Elizabeth's infection. The blooming of their love brought with it the seeds of death.

So the millionairess novelist, after decades of popular success but intellectual derision, now finally revered by her peers as a truly creative figure, has reaped the ultimate harvest of her experimental invest- igations. And she's dis- covered that no amount of money can buy her a reprieve from the haunting harbinger of doom.

She was born Eliz- abeth Smith in the small country town of Godal- ming, the daughter of a surgeon and his wife. An only child, she soon found that inventing playmates and characters filled her lonely life. At Roedean school she did very well in literature and went to Homerton College, Cambridge, where she developed a repu- tation for journalism on *Varsity*, the university newspaper. She was a popular undergraduate, though one fellow student commented yesterday, 'rather refined and snooty — a trifle holier-than- thou'. Pictures (above) show her as a plump, pleasant, beaming girl with chubby cheeks and rolls of puppy fat.

On leaving with a Master of Arts degree, she rapidly acquired a secretarial position and was then promoted to the position of sub-editor on the *Guardian* newspaper, but she spent her leisure hours refining her literary skills and it wasn't long before her first work, *Divine the Lady*, was accepted and became an instant success. Ever since then, she's led the life of a career novelist, churning out nearly 30 big-selling books on a regular basis, one a year on average. As her popularity grew, she started hitting a million copies on every release. Her international status grew and her novels were translated into hundreds of languages. The profits allowed her to buy the lovely old house Willings where she has lived alone with her dogs, a confirmed spinster until her recent wedding. Well known in the villages and surrounding area, she has become a popular local celebrity, opening fêtes and frequently spotted in the shops and pubs of the Surrey towns. A sturdy, suited, tweedy lady (above), admired, re-spected and liked.

Now 51 years old, her friends say they are distraught at this un-expected surprise devel-opment.

'It's so awful,' says one of her closest confidantes. 'Kirk and Elizabeth were so happy, the perfect couple, a dream come true. They were looking forward to many decades together. I've never seen a more contented pair. And then, out of the blue, this ghastly news. Totally undeserved.'

Unfortunately, it was not totally undeserved, though. Our top reporters uncovered a tangle of sordid relationships and brushes with the law that have made Kirk Kurabbi a regular visitor to the notorious prisons of Morocco. His life of petty crime before meeting Elizabeth virtually guaran-teed his acquiring the virus now passed on to his poor, unsuspecting wife.

The novelist Henry R Hathaway, himself a frequent visitor to Tangier and a published author of some stature, told the *Daily Mail,* 'It was pathetic and frightening to those of us who considered ourselves her friends. This vile little man appeared to set out to seduce her and she, poor lady, simply could not accept the truth. Everybody in Tangier believes that Kurabbi is a fraud, a criminal and totally immoral in every way. We tried to warn her but she simply would not listen. It's all very, very sad.'

On being contacted for a response, Mr Kurabbi declined to comment.

It's all a miserable moral fable for our time. The only safe way to conduct your life is to stick to your own society. The thrill of indulging in forbidden experiences may seem to enhance your life, but, in reality, it can end it. Proceed with caution, especially when involving yourself in holiday romances.

Twenty-Four

*L*isa the Teaser was dismayed by the state of her old friend and client.

Elizabeth was propped up in her bed, pillows under her back and arms. She was transparently thin with gaunt black patches under her eyes. Her face looked like a skull with the skin stretched taut across the bones.

But the saddest aspect was the acceptance.

Lisa could see that Elizabeth had ceased to battle. Although the peace was comforting, the inevitable welcome of death was frightening.

'I've been through it all. The pain isn't too bad, thanks to the pills. The anger has gone completely — what's the point?

'In many ways, I'm simply grateful for the months of happiness and the years of contentment before that. I wonder what's coming next — if anything. I feel sorry for Kirk. Not only has he been robbed, too, but he's got this to look forward to in a few years as well.'

Kirk had kept the papers away from her, and he, the servants and their friends had managed to thwart the attentions of the press.

Her sight was going. She had bad memory lapses when she forgot who she was. She looked 20 years older, frail and bony, arthritic and unhealthy. She coughed and wheezed. And the smell was dreadful. It was all Lisa could do to stop herself holding her nose. A decaying, rotten, fragrant odour, subtle but invasive, everywhere.

Elizabeth had become a little old lady whereas, a few weeks before, she had been sturdy and fit, plump and rounded.

When the disease struck, it often conquered very swiftly. And Elizabeth had progressed from being HIV Positive to developing full-blown AIDS much faster than most other cases.

Yet still she had kept writing. At the worst moments she had found solace in the tapping of the keyboard. Her visits to the world of fantasy gave her comfort, relief and pleasure. And nobody except Kirk was allowed to read her work.

Lisa tried to sound cheerful, quoted the amazing sales figures for the book, told jokes and chattered about mutual friends but her mind was not in tune with her tongue. It was contemplating the illness. The speed and the strength of that virus. The victory of the enemy over the human immune system.

She had lost several very close acquaintances to AIDS. Some lasted for years, getting better and then worse, seeming to beat it and then slowly succumbing. Others went fast, like Elizabeth. A few weeks of increasing disability. Rapid deterioration followed by death. In many ways, that was better.

But it was never easy, either for the sufferers or those left behind.

Elizabeth handed her a sealed brown envelope.

'I've finished it. *Ramadan Regained*. Kirk has the floppy disk. I've asked him to print up several hundred manuscripts. I want you to have a spectacular dinner after I've gone. The Guildhall. Invite everybody who was involved in the Booker Prize whether they voted for me or not. Seal the entrances. Lock the doors. Make everyone read it there and then. The first time for all of you.'

She smiled painfully. 'I'll be watching from up there, smiling, and possibly even laughing!'

Kirk came into the room with a tray loaded with tea and sandwiches, cakes and biscuits. Elizabeth had totally lost her appetite but the sight alone of the steaming pot and creamy plates lightened the atmosphere in the room. He poured a Wedgwood cup full of Earl Grey and handed it to his wife, gently stroking her as he did so.

'Now you drink that. It'll do you good. Hot

and aromatic. Just crammed with all the tastiest flavours. Bergamot, fresh milk, honey, real leaf tea — what a lucky girl you are!'

She smiled at him. 'Yes, I am, but not for the drink — for you.'

Lisa grinned. 'You two lovebirds! Have you no shame? You're like a couple of teenagers. The Romeo and Juliet of the literary world!'

And, indeed, there was a kind of beauty about the vibrations between them. Love can transform the ugliest gargoyle into the most handsome prince.

Kirk looked at his wife. 'Not long now, darling. Soon it will all be over and there will be peace. It's been a difficult few months, hasn't it? But think of those marvellous times we had. Worth every second, weren't they?'

'Indeed they were. My happiest memories. And everything distilled into two wonderful years. I'll never forget it and I'll never regret it.'

She closed her eyes and slipped away. It was some time before Kirk and Lisa, chatting quietly as they sipped their tea, realised she had gone. And when it dawned on them, their sadness was sweetened by the way of passing. Gentle, unnoticed, undramatic, final.

I'll never forget it and I'll never regret it.

'Not bad for last words,' thought Lisa as they left the room and began the final preparations.

The media coverage was enormous, of

course, and she felt sorry for Kirk, who had to endure the most intrusive and offensive questions and commentary, but he held up magnificently, polite and well mannered, never losing his temper or snapping replies. The funeral attracted hundreds of remote mourners, recent fans and fair weather admirers.

Alone some days later, Lisa picked up the novel and re-read *Ramadan Mislaid* from cover to cover, scarcely pausing for tea. It made her cry but it also made her smile. There was such passion there. Such dawning revelation for the realities of life. It was almost an affirmation of the philosophy Elizabeth had espoused after that first, earth-shaking flight to Tangier. She was longing to read the sequel yet she had respected Elizabeth's final request and thought, quite apart from anything else, that it was a terrific way to launch a new novel.

Even on her death bed, she had been inspired by enthusiasm, love, humour and the prospect of doing something different.

Not a bad epitaph for a life.

Epilogue

*I*t was the most extraordinary launch. Lisa the Teaser had done herself proud again.

The entire Guildhall had been hired and sealed off. It was decorated beautifully and there was a faint scent of incense in the atmosphere. The waiters had been closely vetted. There were dozens of security guards. Those lucky enough to be invited included critics, media taste-makers, television and radio gurus, Press leaders and international publishers.

Each had been given on entry the sealed package marked 'NOT TO BE OPENED UNTIL INSTRUCTED'.

The publicity had been enormous. Rarely had so much print been devoted to a book, let alone a novel, that nobody had read. The Booker Prize connection had increased interest because a recent winner had been made into an Oscar-winning movie — Hollywood suddenly realised that Booker stood for Bookings and not just Books. So the world Press had covered this bizarre event. Stories in the most obscure journals and on the tiniest cable TV stations.

The catering was exquisite. Smoked salmon, *paté de foie gras*, caviar, strawberries, champagne, and, a nice touch, bread and butter pudding from Harvey Nicks.

Lisa had ensured that everyone important had been invited. The publishers were paying for all this — and, for the first time in her experience, they had neither complained nor rejected her suggestions. Indeed, they had contributed extra ideas involving voluntary additional expense — unheard of!

The select few hundred sat in their seats and fidgeted nervously with the brown envelopes.

Ramadan Regained. The sequel. The final work of Leslie Prince.

Once food had been consumed and drink drunk, Lisa, Mistress of the Ceremony, grabbed a microphone and announced that the moment had come.

'Elizabeth made it her express last wish that nobody read a single word of the second Leslie Prince masterpiece until now. You were the people who acclaimed *Ramadan Mislaid* — you will be the first to read *Ramadan Regained*. Please, open the envelopes, enjoy her words and think fondly of a great lady.'

Fumbling nervously, the packages were

ripped open and the manuscripts removed. Silently they read, some with spectacles perched on the ends of their noses, all deep in thought, devoting hours to the study of the sequel to the last Booker Prize Winner. Some had arrived with reference books and files. Others simply brought their eyes. There were smart and casual, awed and amused, fan and foe.

There was coffee and tea available, refreshments for the pauses in between. They had been asked not to discuss or comment until every last word had been digested.

But, very swiftly, the atmosphere began to change. Chuckles, supressed giggles, a lightening of vibration.

For *Ramadan Regained* was packed with every cliché known to man. Bursting with humour, it sent up romance and coincidence and love and lust. It made Barbara Cartland read like Jane Austen. It ripped bodices and crushed sylphlike girls to hairy chests. Birds sang and clouds rushed across the sun. It was the ultimate Elizabeth Regina penny dreadful and to any critic, any expert in literature, any professor of the novel or publisher of class it was, just as she'd intended, total, unmitigated crap.